It Started with a Friend Request

Sudeep nagarkar

RANDOM HOUSE INDIA

Published by Random House India in 2013
Fifteenth impression in 2015

Random House Publishers India Pvt. Ltd.
7th Floor, Infinity Tower C
DLF Cyber City
Gurgaon 122 002, Haryana, India

Random House Group Limited
20 Vauxhall Bridge Road
London SW1V 2SA
United Kingdom

978 81 8400 420 5

Typeset in Adobe Garamond Pro by SwaRadha Typesetting, New Delhi

Printed and bound in India by Replika Press Private Limited

A PENGUIN RANDOM HOUSE COMPANY

To my Mickey and Minnie

Kisi ko paana ya khona apne bas me nahi hota,
Kisi ko badal ke pyaar karna, pyaar ke naseeb me nahi hota!
Sachhi chaahat hai agar usey paane ki,
Toh himmat rakho usey waise hi apnaane ki!

Contents

Prologue

He was sitting all alone, away from the world, hoping for a new morning in his life, thinking about how harshly life had treated him and brooding over what exactly had gone wrong.

He was busy thinking, *When things go wrong, you feel so miserable and all you wish for is to completely erase the bad memories, especially when your intention was never to do wrong. Or was it? Was her death my fault? When things are not under your control, you feel so helpless before your so-called 'destiny'.*

The cold moon was peeking through the clouds floating above Lavasa valley. It was a perfect moment to hide yourself in the arms of your beloved; here he was, all by himself, with no one to keep him company. His fair skin was hidden behind a stubble and his depressed state was visible not only from his sore eyes but his defeated face as well.

As he threw away his cigarette and turned, he saw a girl walking towards him. She was wearing a red top and jeans. He could not see her clearly as she was a bit far off and the fog had lowered visibility. He kept on staring at her to find out who she was. As she came close, he could see that she had left her hair loose. Her face was still not visible. But he felt as if it was a familiar face by the way she walked and the way her hands played with her hair. It was then that he saw her clearly. Her smiling face and her sparkling beautiful eyes made his heart skip a beat. She was his girlfriend, the one for whom he could have sacrificed his life. They loved each other so much that if angels were watching them from heaven, they would have been left stunned.

She came and stood close to him. He was lost in her eyes. He didn't realize when she came and sat on his lap. Their breaths embraced and their lips were only inches away from each other. Then a strange sound fell on his ears and he closed his eyes. Suddenly everything flashed in front of him and took him back to that day when he lost his love, friends, job—everything.

He remembered all the accusations she had made on him—*You are solely responsible for this mess. You deserve nothing better. You can try to be honest to yourself, if nothing else. And if you can't, then go away!* Suddenly everybody was pointing fingers at him. Suddenly he had become answerable to everyone around him. He saw nothing but a dead end ahead.

He opened his eyes wishing to see her in front of him, but there was no one. He searched for her in all directions, wishing to be with her at that moment. He wanted to relive all their memorable moments again, but all his desires evaporated in thin air as he sat in his resigned state. Sometimes he would question himself whether he was really innocent. Or was he the culprit behind all the chaos that had occurred in the last few months?

He was about to light another cigarette when Kritika came and stood next to him, patting him on his back. Kritika was his 4 am friend who always supported him in the worst of situations. She was your typical girl next door, with short hair and a cute smile. She was full of positive energy and could make anyone feel happy even on the worst of days. According to her, the reason behind her charm and beauty was the amethyst crystal she carried in the locket around her neck. She believed it was a symbol of positive energy and could seduce anyone around her. Kritika was one of his best friends, even though they had met only a few months ago. Together they believed that: 'Time cannot define your relationship. It's the bonding you share even if you have met a day before.'

'What are you doing here?' she asked.

'I just want to be left alone. I want to be away from everyone.'

'What will you achieve by doing that? We all know that you are innocent. Whatever happened was fate's doing. You are not responsible for the accident. I am sure you will find some way or the other to prove your innocence. You just have to wait for the right time to come,' Kritika consoled him.

'I really don't know how to do that. It seems as if sand is slipping through my hands and I am watching helplessly.'

'Come on now, everyone is waiting for you at the hotel. It's my birthday.'

Kritika had booked them at the Ekaanth Hotel to celebrate her birthday on February 13.

As soon as he got up, a drop of tear rolled down his cheek. He remembered all that he had been accused of, and that broke his spirit into pieces. He took out his mobile phone and sent a message to Aleesha.

It's hard to describe how I feel now. I want to explain everything to you, but I don't know how to. I feel so alone and I'm scared. All kinds of thoughts are running through my mind. Stress is eating me up every minute. If only you were by my side today, I would have never felt so alone. Our gang has gathered here to celebrate a birthday party and my eyes still search only for you. But alas, you are not here. Do you feel the same pain as I do?

Kritika was watching him, waiting patiently for him to finish texting. She thought of making him understand that everything will be back in its place one day. However, she avoided looking at him as it would hurt him more. She looked the other way round, rubbing her hands, trying to keep herself warm in the cold wind.

It was a starless night. The other couples around him seemed to enjoy the darkness of the night and the privacy it allowed them. It was not the same for Kritika and him though. Kritika was extremely worried for her friend who was looking for a way to bring back normalcy to his life. But they knew that they were trying to climb an impossibly high peak. They were trying to forget the hurt of the past and the fears of the future, wishing his life gets back on track soon, and with it, the smile on his face.

'Thanks, Kritika, for being by my side during this tough phase,' he said feigning a smile.

'Oh, shut up! I know how much you love Aleesha.'

Just the mention of her name was enough to bring a smile to his face. She meant a lot to him and he needed her to support him against all odds. She was the love of his life. He looked back to see whether he had really seen her a few minutes ago. But Aleesha was nowhere around him.

Aleesha

'Aleesha...Aleesha... Your dad just called up to say that the first list of colleges is out,' Aleesha's mom screamed from the kitchen.

Aleesha was addicted to her BlackBerry Messenger and was busy chatting with her friends in her bedroom.

'Aleesha... Keep your phone aside. Your BBM is not going to help you secure admission anywhere. You need a degree in BMM, not BBM. Stop that right away and check the list on the website,' she continued screaming.

Realizing her mom was not going stop till she succeeds in stopping her, she kept her phone aside. She looked irritated at having been asked to stop chatting since she was expecting a confirmation message from one of her friends for a late night house party. She turned on the monitor and logged on to the website. Simultaneously, she also opened a separate tab for Facebook.

Born and brought up in Kolkata, Aleesha was the only child of her parents. They were Thakurs, and her parents saw to it that she was thoroughly pampered. She was extremely beautiful, so much so that no one could ever get tired of looking at her. She was as picturesque as a sunset on the ocean shore. Her eyes twinkled and glittered, her lips were luscious and glossy, and they had the power to mesmerize anyone. Her smile was enough to lighten up the whole of Kolkata. She was like a hot summer's day which could make one sweat. She was not a fashion freak, but knew how to carry herself gracefully. The dimples on her cheeks could give any Miss World tough competition. Not only did she possess looks to die for, she also had equally sharp brains which made her an instant hit wherever she went. She was one of the toppers of her college and had aimed to do her graduation from the dream city—Mumbai.

It was decision day for her. She entered her application number and closed her eyes for a minute, praying for the best.

Nielsen College, Mumbai

Aleesha shouted in happiness so loudly that her mother came running from the kitchen.

'Yay mom, I made it,' shouted Aleesha jumping on her bed.

Her mom gave her a tight hug and went to share the news with her father over the phone. After a long discussion with her parents, it was decided that Aleesha would soon fly to Mumbai and take up admission in Nielsen College. Aleesha's dream was finally coming true and they decided to call for a short family get-together as a success and farewell party for Aleesha.

Relatives and friends gathered at their house the following evening for mocktails and dinner. Aleesha wanted the party to get over soon because she had to join her friends for another party. Aleesha's dad was busy chatting with his friend Mr Kapoor about accommodation options for his daughter when Mr Kapoor suggested Aleesha could stay with his own daughter who was working in Mumbai.

'Don't worry. They say good people and opportunities meet when they are supposed to. As you know, my daughter Tamanna is also working in Mumbai. It just so happens that even Tamanna is looking for someone to share the apartment with. So Aleesha can stay with her, if you agree. I assure you, it will be a safe and secure home for Aleesha,' Mr Kapoor suggested.

Without giving it a second thought, Aleesha's parents agreed to let their daughter stay with Tamanna. They believed that staying with Tamanna would be the best possible option for Aleesha since they had known the Kapoors for almost a decade. Aleesha herself had wanted to stay alone so she could enjoy her freedom and the city nightlife. She had no option but to concede to her parent's wishes. Also, she was in a hurry to leave for the late night house party. An argument there and then would have been a waste of time, which she wanted to avoid.

After all the after dinner formalities were over, Aleesha took their permission to go out with her friends and left with the promise that she will be back for yet another boring family bonding over drinks. She had been waiting for the late night party all evening. It was going to be the last time she was going to meet her best buddies before setting off for Mumbai. After the party, she bid a final goodbye to them, and soon it was time to head for Mumbai.

'Dad, I have just landed in Mumbai. Tamanna is waiting at the arrivals gate. I will call you back once I am settled,' Aleesha spoke on the phone while bringing down her luggage from the conveyor belt.

After collecting her luggage, she headed eagerly towards the arrivals gate. She was searching for Tamanna when suddenly she felt a hand on her shoulders.

'Tamanna Kapoor.'

'Hey. I've been looking for you. What's up?' Aleesha asked with a broad smile on her face.

'Let's leave. The car is waiting. I have to get back to office,' Tamanna said in a rush, choosing to ignore Aleesha's pleasantries. Her cold behaviour made Aleesha feel awkward, but she recollected what her dad had told her, 'Tamanna is an independent girl and doesn't like too much interference in her personal life, though she is very active socially.'

They walked towards the car together. Within a few minutes, the car was cruising on Mumbai's roads.

Aleesha was trying to soak in the city. She poked her head out of the car and let the breeze run through her hair. She closed her eyes as she felt the air on her face. The car halted abruptly at a red light and broke her spell. Tamanna instructed the driver to put on the AC. Aleesha glanced sideways at Tamanna to find her busily working on her laptop. She told Aleesha that she had come to pick her up during office hours and being one of the managers in the office, she had to be on her toes, at least during office hours.

Aleesha wanted to stop the car near the seaside and watch the sunset, but she knew Tamanna was getting late. They finally reached Tamanna's Churchgate apartment. It had two bedrooms, which made Aleesha sigh in relief since that meant she didn't have to share her bedroom with Tamanna.

'Aleesha, you can settle down. I have to leave for office. I will return around 8 pm in the evening. If you want something to eat, then there are some snacks in the fridge, or you can even place an order at the nearby snacks corner. Their menu card is kept on the dining table. Chal bye, I am leaving. Take care.'

Aleesha listened to all the instructions and nodded in agreement.

Lying on the bed, she could not believe that she was finally in Mumbai. She had a quick nap and then called up her parents. After unpacking, she couldn't resist her urge to update a status on Facebook and connect with her friends back home whom she was missing already. She also updated her BBM status.

She dropped a message in the group chat.

I am extremely happy and super excited to be in the city of dreams. But feels like I have left a part of me in Kolkata. I miss baba, maa, and all you guys. Before this day, I never thought that a few hours of separation could hurt so much. Miss you all. Suddenly I find myself thinking about my childhood and the time when I was learning to ride a bicycle. I fell and bruised myself several times but never gave up. You all used to tease me a lot and would make me cry until I stopped. Now I remember all the fun we had during Durga Puja. You all stood by me for so many years which made me strong from within. Here, there is no one yet but yes, if I get my prince charming here, I will surely let you know. Bye everyone. Miss me and if possible, go and see baba and maa. Love you all. Muaahhhhhh ☺

It had been a week since her arrival, but with each passing day, Aleesha kept feeling more and more homesick. She still had couple of days before her college to start and all the admission formalities to be completed. It was Saturday evening and she had convinced Tamanna, who was still not very friendly, to take her for an outing. Surprisingly, Tamanna had agreed, which made Aleesha super excited as she was going to witness Mumbai's nightlife for the first time. She looked in the mirror and thought of what to wear to the outing. She decided to wear a knee–length black one–piece dress with wooden bangles and minimal make up—a little lipgloss and black eyeliner.

On their way, Aleesha asked Tamanna, 'Tamanna di, you must be used to nightlife of Mumbai by now, right?' Aleesha was trying to be not so personal in her questions for she knew by now that Tamanna was a bit reserved.

'Call me Tammy. And yes, I've been in Mumbai for a long time now. But from the last couple of years, if you exclude a few discos and food joints, everything shuts down before 2 am,' Tamanna smiled.

It was perhaps the first time Tamanna had let her guard down in front of Aleesha. Her informality made Aleesha smile. She had made it clear to Aleesha from the first day itself that she was the reserved sorts and didn't like anyone interfering in her personal life too much. So the reply from Tamanna came as a pleasant surprise to Aleesha.

Both of them had a ball during the outing, and spent some good time together at Malabar Hills. They then went to 'The Pizzeria' at Nariman Point for dinner. After dinner, Aleesha insisted they go for drinks at a nearby discotheque. Tamanna thought about it and decided to take Aleesha to the happening 'Thrive' disc in Colaba.

It was Saturday night and the disc was as crowded as the Virar local train. It was full of college students who came in to party late at night, already piss drunk. Those who say there is a certain age limit for drinking will find their perceptions tested once they enter this place. Thrive has an absolutely wannabe-ish crowd consisting mostly of students trying to get a roof to hide from their parents. A first-time visitor to the place will question if girls ever wear jeans or salwar kameez since all one could see was girls in mini-skirts and hot pants.

When Aleesha and Tamanna entered the disc, the scene was no different. It was a typical Thrive weekend night. Smoke filled the air and the teenagers were grooving madly to the latest songs being played by the DJ. Tamanna ordered a drink for Aleesha and herself. Time flew, and soon both of them were three shots down.

Tamanna got a call from office and she excused herself and went outside, as it was impossible to answer the call with such loud music playing in the background. Aleesha was busy dancing and enjoying her drink when an unknown guy came up on the dance floor and started grooving right next to her. She didn't really mind his proximity to her since she was enjoying herself too much to bother and was also under the influence of alcohol.

'Hi. My name is…' shouted the boy, trying his best to tell her his name over the loud music.

But Aleesha couldn't hear a word of what he was saying. Plus, the song being played was her favourite Honey Singh number.

'Is this your first time here? I'm quite a regular here and I've never seen you before.'

'Dude, this style of flirting and starting a conversation is so ancient. Don't try it on me,' Aleesha retorted.

'So you like modern, "Yo-type" guys? Then let me ask you directly—which drink should I get you Miss… May I know your name please? I am…' He was about to say his name when Aleesha interrupted him.

For a moment, they both stared each other and didn't spoke a word. He kept thinking what Aleesha would say. He didn't want to miss the chance of introducing himself to, who he thought, was the most gorgeous girl present in the disc. Her black sequinned dress was shining in the dim disco lights and her skin glowing like a star. Her eyes had that sparkle which was enough to seduce anyone. He already was. He couldn't even utter his own name after Aleesha interrupted him. He just kept staring at her. His name was…

Akash

'Now that's what's called a perfect strike!' Akash exclaimed jumping in the air as he took the lead in the game.

He needed to strike one more pin to win. Akash was a bowling expert in nine-pins. He had won many times before this and was confident that it would be no different that day.

Akash approached the lane taking a 15-pound bowling ball in his right hand. Focussed entirely at the pins in front of him, he released the ball carefully. As the ball touched the pins, he held his breath.

Bang All nine pins went down in one go!

He had won the game, which meant he had won two entry passes to a disc, and that too on a Saturday night.

'It's time to check out some hot girls tonight at the disc. It's going to be one happening night, Aditya. Woohoo!' Akash's excitement was at its peak.

I was equally pepped up and pounced on him in excitement.

Akash was a Mumbaikar who lived *for* and *with* his family. He was working with the RS group, a company located near Oshiwara in Jogeshwari. He had a charming personality and his dimples would make the girls go crazy. His good sense of humour and style always made him a favourite among his friends. Girls especially liked him for he was a very good cook. He was very caring and possessive about his closed ones and extremely polite in nature. Everyone wondered how a guy like him was single. However, the truth was that after his break up six years ago, he had simply decided to concentrate on his career. I was probably his only best friend and he shared everything with me, including the girls whom he fantasized. Akash was a party freak and was all geared up for that night after winning passes to Thrive.

'Aditya, let's go for a movie. We can go to the disc after 11 pm,' Akash suggested and I agreed.

I got into the driving seat of my car and headed towards Infinity Mall.

We were going to catch the 7.30 pm show of the movie *Pyaar Ka Punchnaama.*

Akash took the last row tickets and I followed him inside the theatre. The hall had many vacant seats. Akash eyed the couple sitting in the corner row. The movie began and the opening scene itself was so funny that we were rolling in our seats with laughter.

'Akash, this guy Liquid is so much like you. The way he is cursing his manager is just how you do it,' I teased Akash and laughed loudly.

'Fuck you, asshole. I don't curse so much. That too right after drinking tea,' said Akash trying to defend himself.

As soon as we settled down in our seats, Akash noticed a young girl sitting cross-legged in the front row. He said, 'I wish I get a girl like her in real life. She is so hot.'

I punched him hard on his shoulders and said, 'Shut up, you asshole.'

'I was kidding yaar. Chuck it. Look at that couple in the corner there. It's hardly been twenty minutes since the movie started and they can't get their hands off each other,' Akash said laughing.

'Lagta hai poora paisa wasool karenge,' we screamed which made the couple more conscious. Realizing they were being watched, they broke their intimate stance and adjusted their clothes.

Everyone started making 'ooh' and 'aah' sounds. Poor couple! It looked like they had had enough of their Pyaar ka Punchnaama.

After the movie ended, we decided to eat maska bhurji paav at Khurshid, a famous eatery in Vile Parle. We were regulars at that place during weekends. It was not exactly a restaurant, but more like a roadside stall which was open from late nights until early morning. We reached the place and as expected, it was buzzing with activity. The tables were set out in the open and there was a sizeable crowd in line to place an order. We decided to eat sitting on the bonnet of the car itself.

'Salim bhai, do bhurji paav,' ordered Akash and rested himself on the bonnet of the car.

It was then that I saw a girl with very loud make-up standing at some distance away from the road.

'Look at her. These call girls spoil this place…' I said.

'Exactly. And don't call her a call girl. The high society call girls don't like to be called 'call girls'. They are Escorts.' Akash was completely against the concept of trading your body for money, though he knew very well that most call girls had a sad story that pushed them into the flesh trade.

Within a flash, a Mercedes C-class halted in front of her. The man in the back seat rolled down the window. After a little chat, she sat in the car and left. Eventually, I had to suffer and listen to Akash's long speech on ethics, decency, and morality.

'I agree that all item girls in Bollywood are responsible for girls being treated as sex objects, but aren't these escorts equally responsible for it too? They portray themselves as a sex symbol or a sex toy. You can pay and play with them. And they can roam freely on the roads trying to catch your attention. Because of this, even a well-educated girl, when roaming in shorts or skirts, is looked upon with scorn by our society. But girls need to draw a line somewhere and can't be so irresponsible. With freedom comes responsibility. Why is gold kept in lockers? Why do we have wrappers on candies? That's because every precious thing should be treasured. But why should I waste my time talking about this? As if things will change anytime soon. Forget it!'

Finally, we headed to Thrive, Colaba. It was a typical Thrive weekend night. Since Akash had won free passes, we didn't have to pay a single penny. The cover charges were covered in the pass.

'One flame shot please,' he ordered at the bar counter. The bartender served it with his usual smile. I told the waiter to get me the same drink as Akash.

He lit a cigarette and started tapping his feet to the music. The crowd was going crazy dancing to the rock music being played by the DJ. Akash was losing control of himself due to the effect of alcohol. But he still ordered a pint of beer.

'Drink it on the rocks. Finish it in a go,' I teased Akash.

Akash took this challenge seriously and finished the entire pint in hardly a minute. He somehow tried to balance himself by holding on to my hands.

'Don't challenge me. I can complete any task.' Akash gave a wicked smile.

'As if you are a Roadie. If so, do you see that girl in the little black dress? I suppose she is alone and drunk too. Go ask her name and talk to her for five minutes,' I again challenged Akash. This time, it was serious.

Akash couldn't see her clearly due to the vast distance between them but he could tell she was extremely beautiful and capable of hitting him hard if he misbehaved with her.

'Are you crazy? Just look at her. She is one of the prettiest girls I have ever laid eyes on and am sure everyone in this disc is also checking her out. Man! Just look at her. Isn't she perfect? I can't do this. I can't go up to her and talk. I want my body in one piece when I leave this place. If something happens, neither you nor she will save me. Moreover, I don't have any more paid holidays left,' Akash went on and on until I interrupted him.

'Loser!' I said trying to end the long conversation in just one word.

Akash couldn't take it sitting down now. He took the challenge seriously and started walking towards the girl.

Though his nervousness escalated with each passing second, he approached her nevertheless. She was looking even more sexy up-close. He started dancing beside her. She was too busy dancing to bother about his close proximity to her. Looking at it as the right opportunity, he tried to break the ice. He was now grooving along with her. She didn't oppose, maybe because she was just as drunk as him.

'Hi. My name is Akash,' he said in a low tone. She missed hearing it due to the loud music being played.

He started flirting with her by asking her for a drink.

For a moment, they both stared each other and didn't speak a word. He kept thinking what the girl would say. He didn't want to miss a chance to introduce himself to the most gorgeous girl in the disc. Her black dress was shining in the dim disco lights and her skin was glowing.

'Only if you pay for my drink…which means I get to save on my pocket money. But don't try it on me, mister,' she said and they both started laughing.

'I'm Akash,' he said bringing his hand forward for a formal introduction.

'Aleesha Thakur.'

Akash was mesmerized by her voice and the way she talked. He was lost in her eyes, which seduced him to an extent that if he had been one more pint down, he would have kissed her right there. Somehow, he controlled himself. Her touch was enough to floor him. I was watching the entire act from a corner, which by now had transformed from an act into an attempt to know her better.

'You don't seem to be a Mumbaikar. Where are you from?' Akash enquired.

'I am from Kolkata. I am here for my graduation. I just took admission in Mumbai for a BMM course,' she added further.

'So you are staying here alone?' He wanted to know more about her. All the while, he kept staring at her. He had clicked and framed an HD quality picture of her in his mind.

'No. I am staying here with my family friend Tamanna. Tamanna Kapoor. She is working in Galaxy house in Mumbai as a manager,' Aleesha said finishing off her drink.

In just a few minutes, they exchanged their BBM pins. She had completely taken over Akash's mind by then. Akash didn't want to leave the place but had to. Though he had won the challenge, he had lost something to Aleesha. He couldn't figure out the reason behind the anxiety he had at that time. Was it love at first sight? Akash kept smiling and I didn't miss a chance to tease him. Before moving out of the disc, Akash turned back and his eyes searched for Aleesha but the place was too crowded to spot her. We soon left the place. What a night it had turned out to be.

After returning home, still half-drunk, he messaged Aleesha on BBM. Before she could reply, he fell on the bed with a thud and was soon fast asleep.

Tamanna

'Tammy, do u remember Thakur uncle? His daughter has taken admission in Nielsen College. He was worried about her stay and his concern reminded me of the time when you took up a job in Mumbai. I have told him that she can stay with you. I shall text you her flight details soon,' said Mr Kapoor, Tamanna's dad.

'What? Oh dad, I would have looked for someone here. You know I don't like others intruding my privacy. I mean I wanted a room partner but not a family friend. I wanted someone who would live her life and let me live mine. Now I hope she is not a gossipmonger. I absolutely hate such people. You should have at least asked me once before letting her stay with me.'

'It's okay, Tammy. She won't disturb you. She is a sweet girl. Don't worry too much. I understand your work pressure and all that, but you don't have to be so stressed for such small issues. Chill, my doll.'

Tamanna finally gave in to her father's wishes as she had neither a choice nor the energy to argue any further. Tamanna was of an independent nature and didn't like to compromise as far as her personal life was concerned. She was an introvert and extremely stubborn. She had a short frame with a dusky complexion but her features were very well-defined. She didn't talk much and her reserved nature would often let her be misconstrued as snobbish. It was only her closed ones who understood her feelings perfectly. Her sharp features would get highlighted further when she wore spectacles and it would make her look more intellectual. She usually wore pencil skirts and tops with stilettos and a tightly-tied high ponytail which made her look very strict, almost like a school teacher. She was a manager at Galaxy House, an HR firm, and had been working there since the past one year. She lived alone in an apartment in Churchgate.

Somehow, she convinced herself to let Aleesha into her apartment for her parent's sake but decided to make some things clear in the first meeting itself, so they each knew where the line had to be drawn. She looked at the clock. It was 8.30 am. She was getting late for office and her cab was waiting below her apartment. She took her bag and rushed out.

As she reached the work floor, she looked at her teammates. Everyone greeted her and exchanged smiles.

'Deep, come to my desk in fifteen minutes,' she said in a strict tone.

Deep was an engineer in Galaxy House and worked under Tamanna's team. He had recently joined the company and was on probation. So every time he would get called by Tamanna, it would make him anxious. Deep had the added responsibility of looking after his mother and younger sister since he had lost his dad at a very young age. Since his mom too had retired from her job recently, he was the only breadwinner in his family and could not afford to lose his job. Though he had a fulfilling social life with friends and enjoyed weekends with them, he had added responsibility on his shoulders and this job meant a lot to him. He had his priorities set and was very clear about it from the start.

He went to the washroom to freshen up and then went to Tamanna who was busy signing some papers on her desk.

'Yes ma'am. Any problem?'

'Deep, it's been two weeks since I asked you for the reports and you still have not submitted them! Why the delay?' she said without breaking eye contact with Deep, embarrassing him.

'Just give me a couple of hours and it will be done. I was about to submit it today but got held up with some other work,' he defended himself.

'Okay, cool,' said Tamanna still staring at him.

He smiled embarrassingly and managed to leave. He could sense there was something fishy about Tamanna since the day he had met her. But he kept his assumptions to himself and never discussed it with anyone.

Tamanna turned off her monitor and rested back on her chair. Something was cooking in her mind and it was not the menu for dinner. It was something close to her heart. Due to increasing pressure from higher authorities in office, she had forgotten all about her personal life and had become a workaholic over the years. All this while, she never realized she had drifted apart from her friends and family. She could feel how hollow her life had become. Moreover, her nature of keeping things to herself and not sharing them with others made her feel even more alone. A couple of months ago when she started training Deep and interacting with him, she realized she had developed feelings for him but never told him about it due to her reticent nature. Neither did she discuss it with her colleagues. Her feelings grew stronger with each passing day and she felt like she was suffocating. Suddenly she had developed an urge to touch him and feel him. This urge transformed her from a hard working girl into a desirable animalistic wild lover whenever she was lost in his thoughts.

Relaxing in her chair, thinking about the last conversation with him, she was picturing his body, his tanned skin so close to her that she could actually feel the heat coming from him. His lips wet and moist pressed against hers, his left hand on her waist and the right hand brushing her hair aside so that he could kiss her hard. Every time she thought about his touch, it sent a shiver down her spine. It would turn her on, thinking of him ripping her clothes apart. She concentrated hard on how his touch would feel on her body. She crossed her legs as she imagined Deep's masculine hands removing her top and sliding it up over her head. She even removed one button of her top. Her breathing got heavier and she was about to trace her lips with her index finger when suddenly she got a call on her desk number, which brought her back to the real world.

She came back to her senses and looked around to see if anyone was observing her. Everyone was busy with the day's activities. She breathed a sigh of relief. She got a call from the receptionist's desk telling her that her cab to the airport was ready. She had obtained permission for it a day before.

She buttoned her top, went to the washroom to splash water on her face hard enough to pull her back into the real world. It was getting difficult for her to conceal her feelings. She checked her cell phone for the message from her dad giving her Aleesha's flight details.

She reached the airport and checked the flight status on the big display screen at the entrance gate.

Indigo Kolkata to Mumbai *Arrived*

She was waiting near the arrival gate and observing everyone carefully. She saw a girl looking around eagerly. Tamanna went up to her and kept her hand on her shoulder.

'Tamanna Kapoor.'

'Hey. I've been looking for you. What's up?' Aleesha asked smiling.

Tamanna ignored Aleesha's greeting and directed her to the waiting car. Within a few minutes, they were on their way to her apartment in Churchgate. After reaching the apartment, Tamanna gave her all the necessary instructions and left for work.

Once she returned to office, she found the reports on her table. Deep had submitted it before time. She smiled again, maybe because of the thoughts she had few hours back or because she had escaped a humiliating situation.

A couple of days had passed since Aleesha had shifted to her apartment. She had somehow convinced Tamanna to take her for an outing. It was Saturday evening. Both of them had a ball, spending good time together. Aleesha insisted they go for drinks at a nearby disc. Tamanna gave in to Aleesha's wishes and decided to take her to 'Thrive' in Colaba.

Once in, Tamanna ordered a drink for Aleesha and herself. Time flew, and soon both of them were three shots down. Tamanna got a call from office and she went outside, as it was impossible to answer the call in such loud music.

After finishing the call, she came inside to see Aleesha smiling.

'What happened? Why are you smiling by yourself?' Tamanna enquired casually.

'There was a cute guy who approached me while you were gone. He was not bad, but it's too early to say anything,' Aleesha winked at Tamanna and ordered another drink.

'So where is he now?' Tamanna asked out of curiosity.

'I think he's left. I can't spot him either. Leave it. The night is still young. Let's enjoy. Cheers!' Aleesha said raising a toast.

Both of them looked at each other for a moment and gulped down their drinks in one go. They were so washed out by the time they reached home that neither of them bothered changing into their night clothes. They just slumped down on their beds and dozed off to sleep.

A Date on BlackBerry

After a memorable Saturday night, Akash woke up late the next morning. The night before, he had lost his heart to a gorgeous looking girl. Aleesha. He was still half asleep when he felt like someone was hitting him with a hammer. He soon realized that the throbbing headache was a result of the hangover. He had a bad headache, which meant that either he had had an awesome night or that he was going to have the worst day ahead.

Still in bed, he stretched out his hands fumbling the side table for his mobile. He hardly remembered what happened last night. He wished he had slept for one more hour. The headache was getting unbearable. Everything around him seemed blurred. He finally got up from bed, still thinking about the previous evening. He unzipped his pants and was about to take a leak when he realized he was in front of his window and not the washroom.

'Err!' he said to himself, 'Oh God, I hate mornings. It's the lack of sleep that causes hangover, not drinks.'

He came back to his bed and saw his mobile lying dismantled on the floor. Its battery was in one corner and the cover was under the bed. His body refused to allow him to bend down and pick them. He struggled hard to put his phone together in one piece. He switched on the cell phone and again lied down on the bed covering himself with his blanket when his phone rang.

'Good morning,' Akash said, still hungover.

'You bloody swine… were you sleeping or dead? I called you at least ten times to check if everything was alright at home,' I yelled at him.

'Ya bhai, I am okay. I don't remember much from last night, but the fact that I was about to pee through the window suggests that I had an awesome night,' he managed to laugh.

'Just check your messages. We almost landed up in jail because of you yesterday.'

Akash opened WhatsApp to check my message.

Fuck you asshole! I am sure you have gone off to sleep. Do you even remember what you did last night? I kicked you out of the disc after you flirted with that girl in the black dress. I think her name is Aleesha since you kept shouting her name while walking out of the disc. But you ran straight into the small light post and if I wouldn't have dragged you away quickly, it would have almost landed on your head. You refused to let me drive, got into the car, and took off. From there we went straight down the wrong side of a one-way road. Needless to say, our luck ran out. A cop was waiting for us. When he asked us where we were coming from, you replied that you had killed a girl and her dead body was in the boot space of the car. 'Laash dikki me hai' you had said. Then what, I lost 500 rupees for such behaviour courtesy 'YOU' and we reached home two hours late.

Akash called me again after reading the message and we just laughed on the phone without speaking a word. I just told him casually to check if he had called or messaged someone to avoid leading to an embarrassing situation. Perhaps, I have this habit of texting and irritating people after gulping down a couple of drinks. Drinking was indeed an emotional gateway for men. Akash disconnected the phone and rechecked all the messages. Suddenly, he jumped out of his bed in panic. *Impossible! How could I? I mean how? I mean when? Holy shit I am screwed,* Akash wanted to scream aloud.

He saw that he had sent a BBM message to Aleesha before dozing off. He began cursing himself for the blunder. It had hardly been a few minutes since they met and he had already messaged her saying that she was the princess of his life. It could make her think that either Akash was a big flirt or that the guy had lost his mind after gulping down a few pegs of alcohol. Akash stood speechless and numb, not knowing how to react, and all he could think of was ways to disappear like the Genie of Aladdin. He read the message that he had sent.

At the risk of sounding like a flirt, I want to tell you that I could not erase you from my mind. You came into my life when I was least expecting it. It was as if I had hit a jackpot.

When I saw you, I don't know what clicked, but from that moment, I could not get you out of my head. I always knew that love would find me someday, but never did I know it would come like this. Your touch healed this broken heart and you caught me off guard and took me by surprise. I was initially reluctant to send u a BBM at this hour. Is it too late? Should I send you a request on Facebook? Your profile pic again urged me to send you a BBM. And no, I am not being desperate here. Everything seems so right, so perfect. Oh god. I will go crazy. Aleesha, please don't take me the wrong way. Do reply. I am not so drunk. ☺

Tere golden face ki beauty ne,
Mere komal heart pe attack kiya.
Sabko reject kiya aur tumko select kiya.
Request hai tumse ise refuse na karna,
Dosti ke is bulb ko kabhi fuse na karna!

On BBM, there is a way of knowing if the other person has read your message or not. Right next to the delivery tick mark appears 'D' for 'delivered' and 'R' for when the recipient 'reads' the message. She had not read the message yet. The R symbol didn't show above the tick mark. He thought that she was still sleeping. At the same time, he wondered what she would think after reading the message. He badly wanted to somehow get Aleesha's cell phone and delete the message he had sent or press the undo button on his phone. But all he could do was bite his nails in anticipation of what was going to happen if she were to read it. He kept his cell aside and wanted to run away from the situation.

However, after every five minutes, he checked his cell phone hoping that Aleesha had still not read that message. He would have eagerly expected her reply in any other normal situation, but at this moment, he was praying not to receive any message from Aleesha. When he checked the phone for the twentieth time, he saw the R symbol above the tick mark. Aleesha had finally read the message.

Oh, fuck! Oh, shit! He was really nervous.

Aleesha is typing a message, showed the BBM screen. His eyes popped out of his head and before she could send the message, Akash quickly typed a message and sent her.

I am extremely sorry for last night. Ignore the message. It wasn't intentional. I was just kidding. Don't take it seriously. I was not in my senses.

He tried to hide his panic. He tried his best to make things sound normal for he knew the intensity of the blunder he had committed.

As soon as he sent the message, Aleesha's message popped on his screen.

Hey dude, are you insane? Were you out of your senses? From where did you copy paste it? Don't tell me you were serious! As if it's love at first sight. Two things I love in men—they never stop trying and they never miss an opportunity. Ha ha!

His confidence grew a little. Akash decided to take a chance with the conversation. His fears had taken a back seat.

Akash: *I just tried to make you laugh and I think I succeeded in doing so. I am too good.*

Aleesha: *Huh? Why do you think I am messaging you? Is it because I care? Or because I miss you? Or because you have become my secret crush? No. It's because I need someone for time pass. I am getting a little bored here. :D Rofl. I am the best.*

Akash: *Err… That was rude.*

Aleesha: *I'm just kidding. Chill!*

Akash: *Hmm. I know. But trust me, you were looking lovely last night. You were so…*

Aleesha: *Okay stop.*

Akash: *Stop what?*

Aleesha: *Thinking about me and stop flirting. We hardly know each other. We are not even friends. :P Chalo c'ya, I need to freshen up.*

Akash: *Let's meet in the evening for a cup of coffee. You know, a lot can happen over coffee. Let's give it a try. At least for the sake of our new friendship. What say? Think over it, am not that bad.* ☺

Aleesha: *Nope. Get over it dude.*

Akash: *Oh come on, I am asking you out just for a coffee. You're reacting as if am asking you out on a date.*

Aleesha: *Byeeeee.*

Akash: *Atleast gimme your number so that I can call you.*

Aleesha: *I said byeeeee. :D*

Akash still tried his best to convince her and continued to chat with her for next couple of hours. He finally managed to convince her for a cup of coffee. He knew she was not going to turn him down and was just being a little difficult like all girls are initially. After all, she knew that Akash would keep on trying until she agreed. It happened exactly the way he wanted. Though they didn't exchange their numbers, they finally decided to meet at CCD in the evening.

'Are you crazy? You mean she really agreed to meet you? Cut the crap. Either she was still hung over from last night, or you are a fool to think she cares. Do you think you're Salman Khan that she has agreed to meet you in such a short span of time? Or do you think I am a fool with a big C written on my forehead?' I reacted when he told me the whole story since I felt Akash was bluffing.

'Aadi, shut up. I am serious. You think I am joking? Not at all, yaar. I managed to convince her to meet me for coffee. That's it. I have also told her that my friend Aditya will join us,' Akash said in a very soft tone, as he knew I would burst out in anger after that.

'Akash have you lost it? Or do you want another beer to regain normalcy? Why do you need me there? What am I going to do? Should I eat ice cream while you give her a smooch?' I said wanting to almost bang my head on the table.

Akash had done all that he had never done in his life in the last 24 hours. It was the effect of a girl who had hardly met him. I so wanted to straighten his pants so he could stop all this. But according to him, he was 'in love'.

'Aadi, be serious. Guess what? I have also decided to express my feelings to her. That's why I want you to be my moral support there. Please Aadi. Trust me. I am serious. Have you ever seen me talking about any girl in the past few years?' Akash said trying to change my opinion.

'Akash, enough! I mean, are you telling me that even though it's hardly been a few minutes since you met her, you're in love with her and are planning to propose to her? How could you be such a despo? Think practically for once—you hardly know each other and you expect her to say "I love you too". What if she doesn't turn up?' I screamed in frustration.

I was trying to bring Akash back to the real world. But I failed. Akash had forced me to change my mind and agree with what he was saying. As they say, a person loses himself in love and never thinks about what will happen in the end. He was taking Mother Teresa's saying 'If you judge people, you have no time to love them' way too seriously.

'Every girl loves it when she is treated like a princess. Why don't you propose to her in the same way I proposed Riya? I am sure she will love it,' I winked.

He gave me a not so pleasant smile and warned me to be there on time. His nervousness was so visible by the way he was scripting his proposal. He had planned what to speak and how. All I could do was to keep my fingers crossed and hope for the best outcome that evening.

A lot can happen over a cup of coffee. I wished that 'lot' would work out for Akash and Aleesha. But I knew things could go either way. It was 5.30 pm. Akash's nervousness had made me fear the worst for him. As a friend, I wanted Akash to make a good impression on Aleesha.

'Aadi, I am so nervous. I don't think I can do it. Just by uttering her name, my heart starts beating at an abnormal pace' He was almost shivering.

He had worn a white T-shirt and blue denims. He looked extremely charming in the attire. His gelled hair completed the look, but his nervousness overshadowed everything else.

'Be brave. Be a man! You are the king of this world. You are just three words away from your dream girl,' I tried to console him while on the way to the destination in the car.

Neither of us had managed to smoke on the way. We both soon reached the CCD outlet on Marine Drive. We parked the car and walked towards the coffee house. I kept on bugging him to message her on BBM to confirm whether she was coming or not since he did not have her cell number.

'Have some patience. Here I am extremely nervous and you are fucking my brain out. I have just messaged her on BBM, okay?' Akash shouted.

We sat in CCD and ordered two sandwiches. I was about to take my first bite when I looked at Akash. He seemed as nervous as I was some years back when I was about to propose to my love, Riya. Back then I didn't have the guts to speak my heart out and needed someone to push me. Though I was courageous enough to actually bend down on my knees and express my love, I knew how I felt at that time. All the powers from the entire universe had come together to help me express my love. Akash needed the same power today. I had never seen him so cautious and nervous. He had not chased any girl in the last few years and had solely concentrated on his career. It was in these last few hours that he had actually lost himself. His expressions, body language, nervousness, and his eyes expressed everything. I just smiled. I was happy that he really liked someone and wished that even Aleesha liked him as much.

It had been almost an hour but Aleesha had still not turned up. When I asked Akash, he said that the messages hadn't reached her on BBM yet.

'Yaar, I had told you to take her cell number. How can you be so foolish, Akash? How could you trust someone so much? Don't be so innocent bro. I am sorry but I don't think she will come now.'

'She can't do this to me. So what if we met for just a couple of minutes? The spark that I saw in her eyes was real. I could tell by the way she messaged me that she wasn't faking it. She likes me. Otherwise she would have ignored my messages and would have never agreed to meet me. I can't be wrong, Aadi. There must be some problem,' he said in a dejected tone.

I got up from the couch and gave him a tight hug to make him feel better, all the while wishing that Aleesha would message or call him. We waited and then walked to the parking area and drove back to our respective homes.

Akash was disturbed but somewhere deep down he knew it couldn't end this way. He had dinner and checked his cell again. He had received three messages. There was one from Aleesha!

`Hi Akash. I am extremely sorry. My net pack expired and I didn't know about it. I thought you didn't message me and had cancelled the plan. By the time I realized that my net pack had expired, it was too late. Sorry to keep` you waiting. I am texting you my cell number. You can call me after an hour or so. Bye. Sorry again.

One message from Aleesha and Akash couldn't control his excitement. He immediately called and informed me that Aleesha wasn't bluffing after all.

Akash waited for the clock to strike 11. It was around 10.45 pm and he thought of calling her up. But he again dropped the plan and decided to wait for another fifteen minutes. Those fifteen minutes seemed never-ending. He didn't want to show how desperately he wanted to talk to her. But he had unknowingly made the mistake by immediately agreeing to call her. He was recollecting all the things he had to say to her. He noted down a few things on his hand so that he wouldn't forget. He seemed to be more cautious this time around and the reason was obvious. He didn't want to lose on an opportunity and regret it later. In the pin drop silence of the room, the only sound audible was that of his heartbeat. If anyone had seen how anxious he was at that time, he would have rolled on the floor laughing. Who notes down things to be said to one's beloved? Akash did. He was just walking in his room repeating the lines in his mind over and over again as if he had a competitive exam to sit for. All the incidents that had happened in the last 24 hours showed that he was in love. Being deeply loved by someone gives you strength, while loving someone deeply gives you courage. He had gathered all the courage to talk to her for the first time after their short meeting at the disc. It was 11 pm. He dialled her number and Aleesha picked up the call.

'Hi. What's up?' Akash asked.

'Just had dinner. What about you?' Aleesha replied in a whisper.

'Me too. By the way, your caller tune is really romantic. Should I sing it for you? I hope you don't mind. Though I am not a good singer, I can sing it for you.' Akash had completely forgotten what he had penned down and spoke what was in his heart.

'Shut up, Akash. Thank God you are not angry. I am extremely sorry that I couldn't meet you in the evening. Really sorry,' Aleesha apologized.

There's no need to be sorry. I am happy you trusted me and at least shared your number with me, Akash thought to himself.

'What happened? Say something.' Aleesha tried to break the silence.

'If you are free on Tuesday, can we meet? It's my weekly off that day,' Akash said giving it another try.

This time she agreed. Akash was convinced by Aleesha's seductive voice that she would not ditch him this time. He couldn't question her anymore. They talked for a few more minutes before eventually hanging up. Akash was on cloud nine and he felt like he was dreaming. Exactly 24 hours back he had met a girl, so beautiful that he instantly lost his heart to her. His heart skipped a beat as soon as he saw her in the disc. He was not the same guy anymore. The brief meeting with her had changed him. Akash had already started planning to make the most of the opportunity and to propose to her. A strong gut feeling was telling him that she liked him too. It was pretty evident in the way she spoke to him. He closed his eyes and fantasized about going out on a date with her. Within a few minutes, he fell asleep after hours of restlessness. He was relaxed and happy at the end of the day as he had talked to his dream girl for the first time on the phone.

Just before going to sleep, he uploaded his status on BBM so that Aleesha could see it.

`You should see my smile when you call or text me! Gn Aleesha. Your voice is mesmerizing.`

Though Aleesha hardly expressed the way she felt and pretended as if she was not looking for someone in particular, the truth was that she wanted their casual meetings to remain a secret, and not let anybody else get a whiff of it.

She changed her status on BBM to: `It started with a friend request.` ☺

Tuesday morning brought along with it a new hope in Akash's life. It was not that he was not nervous, but he took more time than usual to get ready. I was waiting outside his apartment listening to Radio Mirchi in my car. Once Akash came and sat in the car, my first question to him was whether he had confirmed if Aleesha was coming.

'Akash, I am not going to enter CCD until she comes today. We wasted 200 rupees the last time for no reason. We could have had beer instead of eating sandwiches, man!'

'Aadi, I told you the reason why she didn't come. I also told you that since the past two days we have been continuously in touch with each other. Heck I even know her favourite colour by now. It's pink. She also sent me a picture of herself in a pink top. She looks so awesome in it. After all this, you are still teasing my love! I don't expect this from you. And anyway, we are not going to CCD. We are meeting at McDonald's near CST Station,' Akash said.

'Oh cut the crap, for Christ's sake. I am joking. Today you are finally going to propose to her. Else, I will kill you,' I teased him looking at his nervous face.

We reached McD's in an hour and for a change, Aleesha was waiting for us. Akash waved out to her. *Akash was absolutely right,* I thought. She looked ravishing.

Aleesha had worn a pink top and blue denim hot pants.

'Sexy. Hot. Seductive. Freaking beautiful,' I said with a wicked smile on my face.

'I told you. This is not the only reason why I liked her, I love her nature too. Our wavelengths match,' Akash blushed.

He introduced me to her and we took a seat on a vacant table nearby.

'So what will you both have?' I asked them.

'I will have one Mc Aloo Tikki and small French Fries,' Aleesha said looking at Akash and giving him the sweetest smile.

I got up and went near the counter, which gave them some more time to talk. I took out my mobile phone and sent Akash a message on WhatsApp.

Don't waste time. I am taking more time here to give you privacy. Tell her your feelings. Don't be shy or afraid. Go ahead. Yo!

I turned back and looked at him. He read the message and stared back. He slightly nodded his head in nervousness. However, for the next few minutes, he hardly spoke anything.

I was cursing him for his silence and shyness.

`Show your balls, you ass. Speak up! Don't cry in front of me afterwards. Why are you missing this chance,` I messaged again.

`I am trying. But I don't know how to start the conversation,` Akash replied.

I couldn't delay my arrival anymore and got back to the table. I sat diagonally opposite to Akash and Aleesha sat beside him. I looked straight into his eyes and gestured for him to initiate the conversation.

'Should I get ketchup sachets from the counter?' Akash asked Aleesha. She nodded her head and Akash went to get them.

'So Aleesha, how is life in Mumbai?' I broke the silence.

'It's different from Kolkata, definitely. Kolkata shows you a different culture while Mumbai is totally different,' she smiled. I melted looking at her cute smile.

'And how are the people?' I continued with my questions. Akash gave me a tough look when he spotted me being comfortable with Aleesha.

'Nice. Helpful.' she replied in as little words as possible.

'And Akash?' I continued. This was the question I wanted to ask her all evening. The first two questions were just to create a base to reach to this one.

She kept quiet for some time but her silence spoke a thousand words. I repeated my question again and just as she was about to answer, Akash came back.

'So what were you both talking about?' he asked us expecting an answer.

'Does it make you jealous seeing me talk to her?' I said and laughed.

She looked down shyly taking a bite of the burger while tucking back the strands of hair that had come lose. She looked up at me from the corner of her eyes and saw me looking at her. She smiled in agreement to my question.

I blinked my eyes, an indication that Akash felt the same, and immediately messaged him.

`C*****, go ahead tell her. She loves you. Trust me. Don't waste your time. Show her that you are a man.`

Akash looked at me and replied: `I don't understand how some people have the courage to express their love to their crush when I don't even have the courage to ask her for extra ketchup.`

We chitchatted for the next half hour or so and then decided to disperse. I kept on signalling Akash, asking him repeatedly to speak up. But he didn't.

'Hey, why don't you both join me for the freshers party in my college? I can manage to get entry tickets for you. It will be fun,' Aleesha said just before leaving.

'Sure. Why not!' Akash replied and bid a goodbye to her. She left soon after.

We walked back towards our car. No one spoke a word. When you are in love, you dance like no one is watching, sing like no one is listening, and live like it's heaven on earth. Akash did nothing of that sort. From her smile and her positive reaction it was evident that she too loved Akash. I made him understand the fact that Aleesha won't take the first step but will wait for him to speak those golden words which every girl wants to hear. Every girl wants her boyfriend to be different and unique when he proposes to her. Aleesha was no different. Even she wanted it to be memorable.

Love is the feeling of cold in summers. Akash was feeling this love but was afraid to express it. Aleesha was waiting for the moment when her love would give her a passionate kiss and transport her in to a different world altogether.

A Movie During Interval

I was contemplating while drinking a glass of juice in the morning, when I received a message from Akash.

```
Aadi, tell me where can you meet me? We have
to go to Aleesha's college today at 4 pm for
her function. I have planned something really
special for today. I thought on all the points
you had said. You were right. Meet me and I'll
tell you what I've planned.
```

I told him meet me at the *Garden View Bar & Restaurant*. I took the car keys and left for the venue. Akash had reached before me and was curious to reveal his plans.

'Aadi, why did you call me here?' Akash seemed confused.

I gave him a pat on the back and took him inside the bar section. I ordered one bottle of Kingfisher and a packet of peanuts to munch on.

'Akash, the problem with some people when they aren't drunk is that they are too sober. You fall in that category. So drink this up before you reach the college and hit the homerun today,' I said laughing.

'Are you nuts? I have already planned something very special for today. Trust me,' replied Akash hesitatingly.

'Go ahead with your plans. But have a drink or two. And even Aleesha is okay with you drinking. So what's the big deal? You are one lucky chap. When I was with Riya, she didn't allow me to drink at all,' I smiled remembering those memorable days.

I asked him to have a drink. Just one beer and no more since I knew that he would lose self-control if he had more. He drank an entire glass of beer in a minute's time and then sat quietly without uttering a single word. After some time, he looked at me and revealed his entire plan for the evening. It left me speechless. It really proved that he was deeply in love with Aleesha. I wished I had done something similar when I was with Riya. I agreed that his plans were indeed out of the world. Aleesha or any girl in her place would have loved it.

The waiter served him another glass of beer and he finished that in one go too. He closed his eyes and asked, 'Aadi, tell me frankly—did you see me try my luck with any other girl in the last few years? There were so many skimpily-clad girls around us. But Aleesha is different—a beauty with brains. So who wins out of the two—miniskirts or brains? Obviously, a girl with brains wins hands down. Though miniskirts give a damn good fight. I mean Aleesha too wears them, but her brains outshine everything else and I seriously love her for it,' Akash kept bugging me.

'Are you sane?' I enquired.

'Of course I'm sane. I am not as think as you drunk I am,' he added.

I am not as think as you drunk I am! Alcohol was getting the better of him. Though he was a guy who hardly took an hour or two to regain normalcy, I still told him to stop drinking. He agreed and we moved out after paying the bill. I motivated him so that he could execute his plan and enquired if everything was set.

'Yes, everything is ready and I am just waiting for the right moment now. This time I am confident I can do it. Thanks for being with me. I have messaged Aleesha that we will reach in some time. She will come at the main gate to allow us entry,' Akash replied dabbing the perfume kept on my dashboard on his clothes.

He had waited for this day and if he failed to express his feelings today, he would perhaps miss saying it forever. One should not wait for Valentine's Day to express one's love.

'Akash, this is your day. You don't need roses, expensive gifts, or special dialogues lifted straight from a Bollywood movie. All you need is love and passion. You just need to be truly and madly in love. Don't script your memorable moment. Make it real. Speak what your heart says. Go ahead and propose to your sweetheart Aleesha today so that you can celebrate July 7, 2011, as Propose Day every year,' I suggested on the way to the main gate of the college.

As we entered the college, Akash called Aleesha to inform her that we were waiting at at main gate. A few minutes later, she arrived showing her pass to the girl at the gate who seemed like a friend of hers. While walking towards the stage where the function was to be held, Aleesha immediately sensed that we were drunk.

'Drinking during daytime?' she said giving Akash a naughty smile.

'I thought that will help me move my feet better when I dance with you at the fresher's party,' Akash replied looking straight into her eyes.

We went backstage where Aleesha was getting ready for her dance performance before the party. She went inside the changing room while Akash waited for her outside. I went to the nearby cooler to drink water. When she finally came out, Akash's jaw dropped instantly. His heart almost stopped beating and everything stood still for a moment when he saw Aleesha dressed for the performance. She had worn a white top with blue leggings which gave perfect shape to her curves. Her beauty astounded him. She had the style and class which made her a strong contender for Ms Fresher that day. As she came close to him, his breathing got heavier. He wanted to hold her tightly in his arms and take her away from the real world. He was dumbstruck gaping at her beauty. She was standing merely inches away from him.

'How am I looking?' she asked Akash casually. He was still lost in her beauty.

'Sexy,' he said to which she smiled shyly. She handed him a camera and told him to click her pictures during the performance.

When I returned to the spot after drinking water, I saw the intense looks on their faces and the smiles that they exchanged. I instantly knew something was up between them. After exchanging a few words, Akash walked towards me. He seemed super confident and took me along with him to the front row where we looked for a place from where we could see Aleesha perform more clearly.

As the spotlights fell on Aleesha, everyone started screaming loudly and clapping in unison. The guy standing next to us was fantasizing all sorts of things about Aleesha and discussing her with his friends. Akash looked at me and I could see how livid he was. I told him to calm down, telling him it was normal because Aleesha was the centre of attraction at that moment. She danced like she was floating in air. Akash clicked some pictures from his mobile phone so that he could keep her with himself in the photographs at least.

'Aadi, I know there might be many guys here thinking about trying their luck with her. People just see her on the outside and don't know the real her. Not everyone can see what I can see in her. All I know is when I look at her face, I forget my own name too. I find it hard not to stare at her. I can look at her sweet smile the entire day. It's the beauty within her that I see, while others are merely focussed on her physical beauty. I have madly fallen in love with her. I hope she accepts my proposal,' Akash said staring at her continuously while she danced on stage. I just smiled at him as I had no words to say.

The curtains came down after her performance and it was time for the fresher's party celebrations. The anchor came on stage and gave a speech.

'Well, I speak on behalf of all the second-year students here. Just a few lines of how we all feel about this function. I wish to express our happiness towards our juniors today. They represent to us the same hope and challenge as new players in a cricket team or new twists in a good story. Together we can make a terrific team. You, a brand new Ferrari and we, the sparkling black, Ford Model T. So I, on behalf of all the old faces here, welcome the new faces with open hands, open minds, and above all, open hearts. I now sign off for the evening and will let the DJ take over. Have a blast guys!'

Aleesha came towards us and asked Akash about her performance.

'You left me speechless. You really dance well. I think after Punjabis, Bengalis have mastered this art without training. I did feel jealous when the guys around us started staring at you and gossiping about you,' Akash said.

'Thanks. I love your dimples when you smile. You look so cute,' Aleesha replied. It was a clear-cut indication that she liked him too.

'Let's dance,' Akash said taking her hand in his and moving his legs to the tune of the music.

As they both started dancing, they forgot the world around them. They even forgot that they were in a college campus and were dancing passionately and looking continuously into each other's eyes. In between, they exchanged cute smiles, which echoed the lyrics of their love. This continued for some time until the anchor stopped the DJ. He was about to announce the winner of the Ms Fresher competition chosen by the jury members. Aleesha went backstage to collect her bag from the vanity room.

'It's my pleasure to announce our Ms Fresher for this year. This year the crown goes to Ms Priyanka Arya.'

I was disappointed that Aleesha had missed the crown. Akash and I had observed all the other girls present in the party and no one could match Aleesha. She undoubtedly topped the list. The group of guys who were earlier passing comments when Aleesha was on stage screamed Aleesha's name loudly as the winner.

I could hear one of them say, 'This girl is not as hot as the one who danced. I remember the anchor announcing her name as Aleesha. She was fucking hot. If I get a chance to be with her for even a few hours, I would bang her real hard. She is irresistible. Oh man, what a figure she had. She is perfect.'

I looked around to see Akash staring at them in anger. Akash was already drunk and these comments made him lose control. He had controlled himself when Aleesha was on stage, but this time he couldn't. Even I couldn't stop him. Rather, I didn't want to stop him. There are few groups of sick guys in every college who have no respect for girls. Moreover, when they are commenting on your 'would be' girlfriend, you can't ignore it. Akash too couldn't tolerate it and pounced on them like a wild dog. Suddenly the music came to a halt and everyone stood still looking at Akash beating these guys like an action hero. I joined in when I saw a couple of guys holding Akash and trying to hit him. I knew that within a few minutes the organizers would arrive and get hold of us, either throwing us out or pulling Aleesha up for having allowed us wrongful entry. While Akash was still punching the guys left, right, and centre, I called Aleesha, informing her about the incident, and told her to wait outside the college where we had parked our car. My phone thankfully had her number. A while ago, when Akash was facing network connection issues on his phone, he had called Aleesha up from my number. After informing Aleesha I immediately went to Akash to rescue him from the guys. We ran towards the main gate and within minutes, we were outside the college where Aleesha was waiting for us. I lay flat on the bonnet and heaved a sigh of relief. Akash too was breathing heavily due to the chaos that had occurred in the last few minutes.

'What happened? Will you guys tell me something? What made you two fight? Akash look at yourself, you are all messed up,' Aleesha said in a caring tone touching his cheeks with her fingers.

Akash smiled looking at her. Before he could say anything, I interrupted their live romance session.

'Guys, get inside the car. Let's move from here first,' I panicked.

Aleesha opened the back door and got in quickly. Akash did the same. I accelerated the car towards Churchgate station. I looked at both of them from the rear view mirror. We all had panicked and stared at each other through the front mirror. Akash started laughing and we both joined him. It was a hell of the evening and had sent a chill down our spine. I parked the car at the side of the road and looked back.

'I didn't realize that in the chaos you both conveniently sat behind. I don't wanna look like a driver, guys. How mean,' I said jokingly.

'Oops,' Aleesha exclaimed. The next moment Akash got down from the car and came and sat on the front seat. He looked back and winked at Aleesha.

'Where are we going?' Aleesha asked.

'Aditya is going home but we both can stay back. I hope you don't mind. I'll drop you to your home. So don't worry.' Akash said looking back at her.

'Yes sure. But Aditya, why are you leaving?' Aleesha asked me.

'To give you privacy so that Akash won't hesitate getting close to you,' I laughed looking into the mirror. Akash immediately hit me hard.

'Stop it Aditya. You don't have to be humorous all the time. Actually, he has some official work which he can't delay,' Akash said shifting his eyes from Aleesha to me.

Though we didn't speak anything, I knew he wanted to take her out alone so that he could execute his plan. He was still firm about proposing to her. Once we reached my apartment, I gave the car keys to Akash so that if they decided to stay together till late at night, he could drop her safely. Aleesha insisted I join them, but I made up an excuse and got down from the car. Akash had planned to take her to Raghuleela Mall, Vashi, so that he could spend more time with her.

Aleesha came and sat on the front seat and Akash took to the wheel. I bid them goodbye and Akash started driving towards Vashi.

'Sir, have you made all the arrangements?' Akash asked on the phone when he called the manager of Fame Cinemas at Raghuleela Mall. He was in the car with Aleesha and they were on their way to the mall. The manager assured that everything was ready.

'Which arrangements?' Aleesha asked curiously.

'Nothing. Some work related to office. We have an important meeting tomorrow,' he lied. He wanted to surprise Aleesha with his plans.

Akash glanced at Aleesha carefully. Every time he looked at her, he felt like he was falling in love all over again. This was the best phase of his life and if he had not won the passes to the club, he would have never met her. It was on that very day that he fell in love with her. From that day onwards, Akash was a changed man. He never knew he would live to see a better tomorrow. But the day Aleesha came into his life, all his sorrows disappeared. It made him feel like his days of emptiness were over, like she had filled a void in his heart. His days of sadness were a thing of the past now, as he had found his true love at last. She had opened a new window and showed him love like he never knew existed. Akash believed that their love would continue to burn bright.

He thought of holding her hands while driving but dropped the plan and decided to wait for the right moment. They reached Raghuleela Mall. Aleesha still didn't know what Akash had planned for her. She knew that Akash had decided to take her for a movie but she still couldn't understand why he had planned to take her to a venue so far when there were better options in South Mumbai. She asked him again.

'Have patience, dear. I want to make this the best day of your life. I'm keeping my fingers crossed. Hope you like the surprise,' Akash replied while taking on the escalator.

'Surprise? What kind of surprise? You said we were going for a movie. What can be surprising in a movie?' she asked. Her questions were never-ending.

'Ssssshhh,' Akash said and kept his finger on her lips to put a full stop to her questions. Her lips were soft, like honey dew. He was so lost in her eyes that he kept staring at her with love without removing his finger from her lips. Finally realizing he had been staring at her for way too long, he quickly looked away. When he saw Aleesha taking her eyes away from him, he kissed the same finger with which he had touched her lips. He felt like he was kissing her for the first time and the divine feeling of their 'first kiss' made him go crazy. He wanted to hold her by her waist and dance. He wanted to keep his hand on her lap in the darkness of the cinema hall. But he knew he had to wait a little more.

'Akash now can you tell me? The movie is about to begin. Don't test my patience, please,' Aleesha said trying to convince Akash to reveal the surprise he had planned.

'Just enjoy the movie, Aleesha. Don't think about it so much,' Akash replied.

After an hour into the movie, Akash excused himself and went out of the hall to give a final touch to his plan.

'I will be back. I need to use the washroom,' he said to Aleesha and slyly moved out.

Akash went outside, had a talk with the manager for the final time, and confirmed whether he had received the payment. The manager nodded and said everything was ready and that he needn't worry about anything. Akash watched the clock and asked him the time left before the interval.

'Fifteen minutes more, sir,' the manager answered.

He went inside and sat quietly on his seat. He glanced at Aleesha who looked back at him and gave a smile. She seemed curious to know the surprise. She had somehow realized what was coming ahead, but wanted the event to unfold on its own. She was equally nervous since she was expecting something special.

Their eyes were glued to each other and they spoke a thousand words without actually saying anything. Akash understood her expectations and even Aleesha understood that Akash was really going to make it special. For the next few minutes, they kept looking at each other, forgetting all about the movie. Slowly and steadily, they were coming close to each other, with neither of them realizing it. Their foreheads almost touched each other but they still didn't speak a word. Akash lifted his hand to touch her cheeks. His heart breathed heavily and he could sense the same feelings in Aleesha's eyes. Their face tilted and they almost kissed each other. Their lips were inches away. His palm was about to touch her cheeks when the lights came on.

Interval

Immediately they moved back to their original position and acted as if nothing had happened. Aleesha started curling a strand of her hair with her fingers while Akash stretched his body pretending to relax. They looked at each other and exchanged innocent smiles.

'Don't move. I'll be back in a few minutes with your surprise,' Akash said getting up from his seat.

'What's it, Akash? Come on. Tell me. Where are you going?' Aleesha almost pleaded this time. She was losing all her patience. Akash blinked his eyes and asked her to wait for a moment.

Aleesha took out the Bisleri water bottle from her bag. Just as she was about to take a sip, she saw her name flash on the movie screen. She could not believe her eyes.

Is that real? I mean how? Why? What's next? Is this the surprise Akash was talking about? Did he go outside for this? Her mind was preoccupied with these thoughts while her eyes looked for Akash. He couldn't be seen anywhere. She looked back at the screen and didn't dare to look anywhere else. She felt like her heart had stopped beating.

Aleesha! Aleesha! Aleesha! The text appeared on the screen.

I don't know what will be your reaction after watching this short movie. But I am sure you won't hit me. The text flashed on the screen one after the other.

I've always been someone who is always at a loss for words. But, today I felt like telling you everything to lighten my heart. It's for the very first time in my life that I am taking this step and have dared to do something like this. I would like to tell you that you have wooed me from the very first meeting. I want to let you know that I am madly in love with you and I promise you that I will do my best in making you feel loved and secure with me. I don't know what you think of me, but you really are very special for me. According to me, you are the most beautiful girl in this world. Megan Fox is no match for you. The stars lose their shine when I think about your smile.

I've seen dreams of me kissing you and have spent lonely nights thinking of you. If only you could hear my heart's voice, you would have known that I will love you like no one else. The days have passed since I feel your love in every song. Now it's time to say what I have kept hidden for so long. I want you to stay by my side. Aleesha, I love you! I love you so much that I cannot express it enough. I have a small surprise to let you know that you are my life. I have never felt so good.

A photograph of Akash and Aleesha appeared on the screen with '*Made for each other and together forever*' written on it.

Akash was standing near the entrance door and observing Aleesha all through the clip. Her happiness knew no bounds. She came down immediately when she saw Akash standing near the screen. She stood in front of him. They looked at each other for a moment. Akash was the first one to break the silence.

'You won't say anything?'

'I am speechless, Akash. When did you plan all of this? I never expected that someone would ever do this to me. I am flattered. I still can't believe you actually did this. You had kept our photograph too, the one which we had taken in McDonald's,' she said, and Akash came close and held her hands.

'I wanted to tell you about my feelings in person, but thought of making it special and memorable. I always feared telling you about it because I feared losing you as a friend. I consider myself really lucky to have a friend like you. But now I want to tell you the truth. Each moment away from you feels like a thousand deaths. I would rather lose you and live in sorrow than spend the rest of my life wondering what if...' Akash stopped for a moment and said, 'I hope you will not hate me. But what choice did I have? You are the most wonderful girl I have ever met and not falling in love with you was never an option for me. I love you, Aleesha.'

He had finally expressed his love and he felt on top of the world. Aleesha kept smiling and looking at him with intensity. Without further delay, she hugged him tightly. The moment they hugged, everyone in the hall applauded. It was then that they realized they were in a movie hall. The last few minutes had taken them into a world which many only dream of. They didn't wait for the interval to get over. They left the movie hall to spend some time together before the day came to an end. Akash again thanked the manager for executing his plan to perfection.

Akash started the car and kept one hand on the steering and the other on Aleesha's shoulder. Aleesha too rested her head on his shoulder. Akash gently kissed her forehead and continued driving.

They had almost reached the bridge in Mulund which connected Navi Mumbai and Eastern Express Highway when Akash stopped the car at the side of the road. He sensed his phone was beeping. He attended the call and was about to start the car when Aleesha insisted him to wait for some time. Akash switched on the car's radio.

'I just want to see you so that I can dream about you tonight. I love you Akash. I never thought I would love someone whom I had never even met a few months back. But unexpected things happen and that's life,' Aleesha said kissing Akash's hand.

'I love you too. It feels so nice and secure to hear those words from you. Always be with me.' Akash kissed her hands and pulled her cheeks, which made Aleesha blush.

Akash increased the volume of radio as his favourite song was being played. He grabbed the opportunity and dedicated the same to Aleesha.

Seedhe saadhe saara sauda seedha seedha hona jee,
Maine tumko paana hai ya tune main ko khona jee,
Aaja dil ki kare saude baazi kya naarazi...
Aa re aa re aa re aa!

Sauda hai dil ka yeh, tu kar bhi le,
Mera jahan tu baahon me tu bhar bhi le,
Saude me de kasam, kasam bhi le,
Aake tu nigaahon me sawar bhi le...

After the song ended, Akash sensed the intensity of the moment, switched off the headlights of the car, and switched on the parking lights. The glasses were tinted which made it safe for them. She was waiting for Akash to kiss her. Akash was nervous. He was so close yet so far. The sound of parking lights was the only sound audible apart from their breaths. She had closed her eyes.

Gosh, how on earth can it be so easy for her? Akash couldn't understand it.

He couldn't stop thinking about how he was going to kiss her. He was pretty sure that steam would erupt from his ears if he held her tight and tried to kiss her. He was extremely nervous. It was his first kiss. Aleesha was ready for it. She still had her eyes closed and could feel Akash's breath inching closer to her. Akash looked outside the window. It was late evening and the street was quite dark. He had to kiss her and she was waiting.

Why couldn't she make the first move, he thought to himself. 'I love you' said Akash and turned towards her. He wrapped his right hand around her and kept his left hand on her shoulders, bringing her closer to himself. She leant on him while Akash stroked her back. Finally, their lips met. It was their first kiss in a car on a roadside with no one watching them. He started licking her lower lip and gesturing her to open her mouth. When her lips opened, he slowly pushed his tongue inside her mouth and gently explored it. He placed one hand tightly on her neck and the other one on her cheek. She lightly bit his lip and rolled her tongue over his lower lip. Their hands explored each other. He pushed his hands inside her top while Aleesha massaged his thighs gently. Akash's hand searched for her bra strap when Aleesha opened her eyes and resisted.

'Not now. This is not the right place,' Aleesha said releasing herself from him. They were completely exhausted and out of breath. She smiled looking at him and gave another small kiss.

Akash had pushed his seat back to get some leg space and Aleesha was resting her head on his lap. Akash played with her hair and kissed her forehead. Throughout the journey, Aleesha kept on kissing his neck and biting his ears. He dropped her home and returned. He got down the car and searched for his mobile.

July 7 had indeed become memorable for both Akash and Aleesha. Akash had expressed his feelings in the most perfect way possible, and Aleesha was floating on cloud nine. She wanted someone exactly like Akash who could cross all limits for her to make her happy. Their destiny had brought them together. Their lips met as if their souls were meeting. Even when Akash closed his eyes on his bed, he could feel Aleesha's juicy lips and the tender kiss they had shared. Aleesha too kept thinking about her first kiss that was as memorable as the first Filmfare award that an actor receives in appreciation of his work. She kept blushing all the time whenever she thought about him.

Before they slept, they both changed their BBM status to the song they had sung in the car.

`Aaja dil ki kare saude baazi kya narazi… Aa re aa re aa re aa!`

Coffee on the Rocks

Tamanna had managed to reach office early as she had to submit some reports to her senior officials. No one from her team had come in yet. While she was busy taking printouts of the reports, she remembered she had to take her medicines for hypertension. She went and filled her glass with water from the cooler and after taking her prescribed pills, she walked through the passage towards the washroom.

As she went closer, she could hear some strange sounds coming from within. It scared the hell out of her. But with heavy steps she decided to move ahead. Soon she realized that the strange sounds were of someone making out in the washroom!

'Ooh yeah! Mmm…that feels so good!' a voice muttered from inside the washroom.

Tamanna was standing just outside the door trying to hear carefully what was being said.

'Oh dear, you're too good.' It sounded like a guy's voice this time.

She was stunned to hear a man's voice coming from the ladies washroom. She couldn't believe all this was happening in office. Though flirting was quite common, especially during appraisals, this was something new to her. Someone was actually making out in the washroom! She didn't have the guts to open the door and stood outside silently.

'That was so satisfying, baby. Get up, let me put on my clothes before someone walks in on us,' the girl muttered again. Tamanna kept wondering whose voice it was.

The moans eventually stopped and there was complete silence for the next couple of minutes.

Tamanna thought of opening the door when she heard the girl say, 'I don't think anyone's out there. I'll go first. Don't come out for a few minutes after I'm gone. I'll give you a ring on your phone signalling everything's clear and then you can come out.'

Tamanna quickly searched for a place to hide and found a spot behind a pillar. She heard footsteps ahead of her and tilted her head slightly to check who it was.

Oh, fish! That's Kajal! Is that why she's been getting leaves and incentives without even doing her work on time? Tamanna thought to herself. She stood there for a few more minutes to clear all her doubts. She was not wrong. The guy was her senior Manager, Mr Verma. He was in his mid-thirties whereas Kajal had just graduated. She had joined the company only recently but took full advantage of her senior, knowing that he was addicted to sex. Tamanna imagined what it would feel like to be with Deep in the same situation and ignored the wrong things that happened in office. Deep was still on probation and his leaves, HRA, bonus, and other benefits were in Tamanna's hands. She had a huge crush on Deep and wanted to be in a relationship with him in spite of him being her junior. Though she had never shared her feelings with any of her colleagues or friends, the same thoughts kept revolving in her head. She thought that even though she was hiding her intentions from others, surely Deep had a hint about her feelings for him, but he didn't say anything.

She was drinking water when her phone rang.

'Hello beta, how are you? This is Mr Dalal this side.' Mr Dalal was the owner of the house where Tamanna and Aleesha were staying.

He continued, 'I wanted to inform you that I am looking to renovate our flat. Actually, I am moving to my hometown in a year and thus I want to sell my flats and properties before moving out of Mumbai. So I thought of renovating the flat so I could get a better deal for it.'

'But uncle, I can't shift in such short notice. I need at least a fortnight,' Tamanna requested while on her way to the cafeteria.

'It's okay. Try and adjust somewhere else for a month. Once the interiors are done, you can move back in. In fact, why don't you leave all your furniture in the flat and carry only the necessary stuff?'

Tamanna reluctantly agreed and disconnected the call. She thought of how Aleesha had just shifted and telling her to look for some other place would be really awkward. However, Tamanna had no other option. She had to now find a new residence on such short notice. She remembered that a few of her colleagues lived in rented apartments and thus thought of shifting to one of them for a month. She called Aleesha to tell her about it but her phone was not reachable. She decided to inform her after reaching home at night.

In the meanwhile, she had completely forgotten that she was in the cafeteria and that the counter boy was waiting to take her order. She was jolted from her state by Deep who was patting her shoulders. He had been standing right beside her all this while and, preoccupied in her thoughts, she didn't hear him come. As she felt Deep's touch on her shoulder, her world came to a standstill.

'One Maggi and one apple juice,' she said regaining her composure.

While walking back with her order, she greeted Deep formally. Deep returned the greeting. He took a bottle of Sprite, searched for his mobile, and called up his friend.

'Guess what? She again gave me an overfriendly smile. Oh God, I feel so embarrassed when she does that. I am not the type of guy she thinks me to be. I don't like to use people for personal pleasures. The rumour doing the rounds is that a girl from the other team has crossed all limits to impress her manager. She now gets uninformed leaves and other benefits as well. Even I can get all of these and you know that I am on a third party payroll. So showing personal interest in my manager can actually be beneficial for me and help me in many ways. She has the power to get me on direct payroll but my heart doesn't agree. Even though I need appraisals desperately, I disapprove of those who take the shortcut to achieve their dreams,' Deep told his friend in one go.

'It's a rather tricky situation. Don't ever be informal with her. It can send her the wrong signal. But also don't hesitate to smile and say a few nice words to her whenever you meet her. After all, she is your senior,' the other guy on the phone said teasingly.

Deep knew there was some sense in his words. He didn't want to lose his job by making it obvious through his cold behaviour towards her. He disconnected the call.

Deep was a good looking man with a strong built, good enough to charm girls. He had impressed the people in office by his dedication and hard work. He was strictly professional during office hours and never shirked from his work and responsibilities. He had dreams for himself and his family. The dreams also included his future wife though he was not married yet. However, he was against wrong ways of earning money or getting appraisals. He hated politics and manipulation in the corporate world. If it was in his control, he would have forced everyone to follow corporate ethics. But he knew that the real meaning of office ethics was only in management books, which provides a good read but is never actually followed by anyone.

'Hey, do you have a back up of our project files? Remember, I had told you to save it when I had shared it with everyone?' Tamanna enquired. She was on the phone with one of her teammates.

'How can you be so careless? Just check who has it and give me a call immediately. The system has crashed and I am still in office,' Tamanna shouted.

She hung up the phone and called a technician to check on the matter. It was already 8:30 pm and it seemed like she would take at least a couple of hours more to finish with work. She had already checked in early today and this sudden issue made her wait even after the office hours, which irritated her. But she was helpless. With higher positions come more responsibilities and thus Tamanna had to wait until the issue was resolved. She was having a cup of tea in the cafeteria when her phone beeped. Her heart skipped a beat looking at the caller's name. It was Deep!

'Hello,' she greeted him after picking up the call.

'Hi Ma'am. A colleague just told me about the issue you are facing. I have the backup files with me. If it's urgent, I can reach office in a couple of hours. Should I come?' Deep asked concerned.

'Please do. I'll be waiting. Please try and come as soon as possible,' Tamanna responded.

Deep hung up the phone and quickly had his dinner. He knew he was not going to be paid extra for helping her out but it would certainly help in making an impression on her and might result in rewards in the future. He reached office around 11 pm. There was no one on the floor except the technician and Tamanna. Both of them were engrossed in resolving the issue and didn't notice that Deep had reached.

Deep broke the silence and said, 'I had no idea something like this would turn up. When I got a call, I had just reached home. Therefore, it took me time to come back again. I am so sorry.'

Tamanna just smiled and took the pen drive containing the backup files.

'I hope you had a peaceful sleep last night because I am afraid it will take at least 4 hours to restart the system again,' the technician responded.

Deep wanted to bang the system on the technician's head. He now had to stay back until early morning and had to also be on time for the next day shift. He scratched his head and looked at Tamanna with a raised eyebrow. She thanked Deep for coming on such short notice and told him she appreciated his efforts to stay back until the issue got resolved. After a few hours, the technician restored the system and left. Except for the security guard, the only people left in office were Deep and Tamanna.

After almost an hour, Tamanna asked Deep to join her for coffee while he was busy checking the files on the system.

'Ya sure, should I go get it?' Deep asked.

'No, no. It's okay. You carry on,' Tamanna said and walked outside towards the coffee vending machine.

She looked around the office and saw no one was around. She took two cups and placed one on the coffee machine. As the cup was being filled with coffee, she remembered the morning washroom incident. She felt a sensation run through her body. Suddenly, she felt a hand caressing her back, slowly but passionately. She stood still and closed her eyes. After a few seconds, the hand pulled out the shirt tucked in her pencil skirt and reached for her bra strap. She let out a moan, turned around, and opened her eyes to come face to face with the person. To her shock, there was no one around. She couldn't believe it. She then looked down to see the coffee spilled all over the vending machine. She again turned to see whose hand it was but found no one and realized how desperately she wanted someone to love her. The coffee was still spilling out of the cup. She turned off the main switch of the vending machine.

Damn! The vending machine too had to malfunction now! Fuck man, she thought.

She took both the cups and went back to see Deep still working on the system. She smiled wryly thinking of the morning incident and kept the coffee cup on the desk.

'Thank you so much, Deep, for all your help. It would have left me in immense trouble if I hadn't fixed this issue tonight. Maybe we would have lost this project or the company would have faced huge loses. Then they would have shown me the door and asked me to get out. I am really grateful to you for all your help today,' Tamanna said sipping her coffee in relief.

'It's okay, ma'am. For me, work is always the first priority and this was quite a serious issue,' Deep smiled.

'You can call me Tamanna. My close friends call me Tammy. You can too. After all, you saved my job.' She was trying to break the ice between them.

'Sure Tamanna. Oops! Tammy,' Deep smirked.

'I hope you are aware that tomorrow evening our team has organized a party,' Tamanna asked.

'Oh yes, I will be there,' Deep responded.

Even though Deep was getting increasingly friendly with Tamanna, he knew he couldn't cross his limits. With no one around, Tamanna was enjoying Deep's company. It was almost like a date for her. She called it their 'first date in office'. They chitchatted on various topics until the issue was resolved and then called it a day. They winded up all the work around 4 am and then called the security guard to get them a taxi. The security immediately called a cab to drop them home.

'Be safe and drop me a message once you reach home. Thanks again,' Tamanna smiled before getting into the car.

She smiled all the way back home. She had spent some wonderful hours with Deep. Once home, she opened her notes on her Galaxy Tab and scribbled:

Sometimes I wonder how I feel about you. Sometimes I am scared of these feelings, as I don't know anything about you. Still the dreams about you are so vivid and clear that I feel true happiness and my fear disappears. People say dreams have an underlying meaning to them and one should not ignore them. But as I wake up from my dream, I feel alone. You don't realize what I feel for you. I want you to hear my heartbeats, feel my body, and see my face to understand my love for you. I fantasize your strong arms around me and that makes me feel so safe. Your warm loving body scent sends my heart spiralling out of control. I wish you knew what you do to me. You make me daydream in office and fantasize about you. However, in reality I am all alone without you... It's the fire of love and it won't stop burning unless I feel you and your love. One day you will be mine, I will make you mine...

Four Seasons to Cloud Nine

Tamanna had reached the party venue while Deep was in the lobby downstairs. The party was at the Four Seasons hotel in Worli. The venue was the Aer lounge located on the 34th floor. Deep was escorted to the elevator which went straight up to the 33rd floor of the hotel. Once he was out of the elevator, he climbed another floor through the glittering stairway with small mirrors on the walls that lead to the lounge. It was an open roof lounge with the most beautiful view of the city— including Haji Ali, Mahalaxmi Racecourse, and the Bandra-Worli Sea link. Deep went towards the sea facing side where the cool breeze from the Arabian Sea greeted him. His jaw almost dropped looking at the amazing view. He then searched for his teammates and Tamanna. They were sitting on the opposite side with drinks already served on the table.

Deep took his seat after greeting everyone.

'What will you have?' Tamanna asked.

'I'll take prawns and a cocktail.'

Tamanna placed the order and offered him a cigarette. Deep couldn't deny the offer due to corporate table manners and took one cigarette from the pack. It would have been a different story altogether if he was a non-smoker. However, everyone from the team knew he smoked. Thus, he couldn't refuse and lit a cigarette. He somewhere felt that he was encouraging Tamanna to come close to him and get more personal. He hated that fact but felt completely helpless about it.

After dinner, Deep got up from his seat and moved towards the sea facing side of the lounge asking aloud if anyone wanted to join him. Tamanna readily agreed to join him and got up from her seat. Deep gave a sarcastic smile as she straightened her dress and started walking alongside. She was heavily drunk but Deep ignored this fact. They reached the edge of the rooftop which had a long glass boundary. Tamanna had been silent all through the walk and didn't even look at Deep. He sensed something coming his way after the long silence. He had almost finished his cigarette and still Tamanna hadn't uttered a word. She was too drunk to be in her senses.

'Are you okay? Deep enquired. Her long silence was making him uncomfortable.

'Can I ask you something?' Tamanna said staring at Deep. She was finding it difficult to even stand on her feet.

Deep held her hands and made her sit on the nearby couch. A smile popped on Tamanna's face. She held his hands so tightly that Deep could hardly move his fingers. He was shocked with Tamanna's strange behaviour. He hadn't expected something like this to happen. He tried to free his hand from her clutches but failed to do so.

Deep gave up eventually and said, 'Tammy, You should leave. You are drunk and it's getting late.'

'No. I am not drunk. I am okay. Deep, you are really very cute. You always take care of everyone and I love you for that... You should...' she muttered but Deep interrupted her by making her stand and signalling to one of his teammates to help him out. When everyone saw her condition, they made her sit on the couch and tried ways to make her regain normalcy so that she could at least reach home safely. However, she was in no mood to listen. She closed her eyes and rested her head on the couch. Everyone asked Deep to take her home safely since she was not in a state to go alone.

Deep knew what could be the consequences if he went alone with her. He was already scared and shocked with what had happened a few minutes back. Nevertheless, he did not have any other option. There were two managers requesting him to do the honour and Tamanna continuously muttered his name when they asked her who they should get in touch with to help her reach home safely. Deep took her bag and they both walked down the staircase. Tamanna took the support of his shoulders to walk. She kept on muttering Deep's name until they reached the lobby. Deep made her sit in the lobby and asked the gaurd to call for a taxi for them. She held Deep's hand and walked towards the taxi. He made her sit on the backseat of the taxi and was about to close the door and move towards the front seat when Tamanna whispered:

'Please don't sit in the front. Sit beside me. I am scared and I need you. Please Deep, it's a request.'

She was almost pleading with him. Deep thought for a moment and decided to sit at the back with her. Looking at her condition, he knew it would have been too harsh if he had sat in the front.

'Bhaiya, Churchgate chalo,' Deep told the taxi driver and shut the back door of the taxi.

Tamanna stuck her head out of the window and shut her eyes, letting the breeze hit her face. It was not very cold outside but Tamanna was drunk and the breeze made her feel drowsier. Deep shut his eyes and felt that he should have avoided this party to stay away from all the chaos. He wondered what the managers might have thought when Tamanna repeated his name continuously in front of them. He didn't want it to be this way. He wanted to stay away from office gossip and not be a part of it. To make things worse, Tamanna held his hand again, but with more passion this time. She almost fell on him when the driver took a right turn. Deep couldn't believe what was happening.

'Bhaiya, aaraam se,' Deep requested the taxi driver as he knew it was no use requesting Tamanna.

Tamanna was still holding onto his hand firmly. She opened her eyes slightly and turned her head towards Deep. He didn't notice her as he was looking outside the window. Tamanna kept gazing at him while the taxi cruised towards Churchgate. She finally broke the silence between them and said, 'Deep, don't leave me alone. Stay by me always. I know you think of me as just a friend and that I'm crossing the line here. But I have to say it today,

I can't take it anymore. I can't stand next to you without wanting to hold you. I can't look into your eyes without feeling that longing you only read about in trashy romance novels. I can't talk to you without wanting to express my love for everything you are. I don't love you like bubbly college girls but I love you as the plant that never blossoms but carries the light of hidden flowers in itself. I have seen dreams where I kiss you...'

Her words not only shocked Deep but also raised various questions in his mind. Deep interrupted her but she was in no mood to stop and continued, '...and I have spent lonely nights when I miss you. It's been so long since I have kept these feelings hidden from you, but I feel like telling you everything that is inside me, I want you. I want you to be mine forever. I've never felt this way before meeting you and my feelings for you increased during your training sessions. I have never had the opportunity to tell you or anyone else about these feelings. And if bringing it to light means we can't hang out any more, then that would hurt me. I don't know what the next moment will bring, but you will always see your picture in my eyes. I love you...'

Deep was stunned to hear all of this. He was clueless on how to react. He somewhere knew that Tamanna had feelings for him, but never thought it was more like an obsession. He always treated Tamanna as a manager and from the past few days, as a friend. It was not that he did not believe in love but he wanted his professional life to remain simply professional. His office hours were dedicated just to his work and work alone. The irony of the situation was that Tamanna was not even in her senses when she was expressing her love. Maybe the next day she won't event remember all this, thought Deep.

She continued, '...where is my Tab, Deep? I have written so many things about you in it. Please let me read it.'

Deep immediately took the Tab which was kept on the seat beside her but Tamanna snatched it from his hand. She opened a saved folder and tried to read out the lines.

Jaane woh meri bekarari ko samajhta kyun nahi,
Jo mujhe mehsoos hota hai, woh use mehsoos hota kyun nahi?
Apne pyaar se seechti aayi hoon main is phool ko,
Mere pyaar ka yeh phool uske dil me khilta kyun nahi?
Har pal uske pyaar ki galiyon mein bhatakti hoon,
Na jane woh bhule se bhi wahan se guzarta kyun nahi?
Maar chuki hoon har ehsaas ko uske pyaar mein,
Ichhaon ka yeh aashiyana fir bhi bikharta kyun nahin?

The taxi halted near Tamanna's apartment. Though he was in shock, he helped Tamanna get out of the car and looked around to make sure no one was watching him. She somehow managed to walk to the gate.

Deep was unable to catch much sleep that night. The biggest question that kept him awake all through the night was 'What next?' Should he forget his principles and take a step forward thinking of all the luxuries that would be provided to him, or should he act as if nothing had happened that night? Though he wanted to call it an end and quit his job, he knew practically he couldn't take that step as he had responsibilities on his head. To fulfil the same responsibilities, should he jump in an ocean of greed by killing his self-respect or respect the dreams that he once saw with his dream girl?

Sealed With a Kiss

No one really loves early mornings after partying hard the night before. The alarm broke Tamanna's sleep. She walked towards the kitchen still half asleep. Aleesha was making early morning tea. Tamanna drank a glass of water and sat on the sofa in the living room. She didn't remember even a second of what she had done the previous night on her way back home.

'Hey, you came in late yesterday. I had called you but your cell was switched off. Tea?' Aleesha asked.

Tamanna nodded and Aleesha poured her a cup of tea.

'Why did you call yesterday?' Tamanna asked while searching for a newspaper and continued, 'Oh shit, I completely forgot to inform you. It just skipped my mind because of last night's party. The house owner had called me yesterday evening to inform that he needs this flat vacant for a month for renovation purposes. In six months' time, he is planning to sell it off. I am extremely sorry but I think you will have to look for another accommodation till then. Even I am shifting to my friend's house for a month. I am really sorry.'

'I think I can stay in the college hostel now since classes have commenced. Don't worry. I totally understand. I will tell dad about the issue and shift to the college hostel as soon as the formalities are done,' Aleesha smiled. Her face didn't show that she was worried. But, Tamanna's sudden decision had shocked her as that was not expected. She called Akash and they decided to meet up in the evening.

Aleesha sent a message on WhatsApp to Akash saying: `Let's meet at Shivaji Park, Dadar, at 7 pm.`

`Sure sexy. Muaahh!` Akash replied.

Aleesha blushed after reading his message and sent him a smiley emoticon. She had bunked lectures that day to complete her pending assignments. She waited for the clock to strike 7 for two reasons. One was that she was eager to meet Akash. The other reason was more critical. She had to discuss with him how she should go about shifting to the college hostel.

She took a cab and left for Shivaji Park. She was wearing a knee length, blue, one piece dress and had left her hair loose, with a few strands falling on her face. She was hardly wearing any make up except a slight lip gloss and blue eyeliner. Within a few minutes, she reached the destination and got down from the cab.

Akash was waiting outside the petrol pump near Shivaji Park. Seeing Aleesha standing on the other side of the road, he couldn't resist looking at her from head to toe. She looked perfect. Akash parked the car and walked towards her. He gave her a sweet flying kiss, which was returned with equal intensity. Akash held her hand and they searched for a secluded place at Shivaji Park. There are only a few places left in Mumbai where couples can spend some quality time together without any disturbances and this was one of them.

Aleesha took out a sketch of Mickey Mouse which she had made for Akash in between her lectures. Akash laughed after seeing it and pulled her cheeks. He loved how innocent she was.

'It's super cute. I will pin it up on the pinboard in my room. Love you so much,' Akash said kissing her cheeks.

Aleesha didn't say anything. Though she managed to smile, Akash could sense her fear. He held her hands, came closer to her, and asked, 'What happened, tell me. I will suggest a solution.'

She narrated the entire story and said, 'I had a discussion with mom and dad too. They have agreed to my decision of staying in the college hostel. Instead of looking for some other place for a month, it is better to shift to the hostel.' She stopped for a moment and rested her head on Akash's shoulder.

'So what's the problem? You are absolutely right,' Akash said playing with her hair.

'The only problem is that from now on, I will not be able to stay with you till late nights. And that's why I wanted to discuss my decision to move out with you first,' Aleesha said leaning closer to Akash, almost on the verge of kissing him.

Akash didn't deny her the pleasure of the kiss. Men will be men, after all. He slowly embraced her and locked his lips with hers. Akash was pretty nervous as he knew other people around them were definitely noticing them. But he decided to ignore them. Aleesha's tender kiss incited him like fresh blood to a shark. He grabbed her by her waist and kissed her all over again. In the moonlight, she looked ethereal, almost like a painting. He wondered how he could have ended up with such a beautiful girl. His girlfriend. His soulmate.

Akash looked sideways and saw another couple doing much more than kissing. Akash stood astonished for a moment, asked Aleesha to move with him to another secluded spot, and found a bench and sat on it. They hugged each other and then Akash asked her to sit on his lap. Aleesha didn't argue.

'Can you just lean on me a bit more?' Akash said with a naughty smile.

Akash kissed her cheeks first and then his tongue nudged her lips to open her mouth. It was another passionate evening for both of them. July 7 marked the beginning of their relationship and their first kiss, and now July 20 would be remembered as the day of the first passionate evening of their life. Their love made them forget the world around them. Soon it was time for Aleesha to leave since it was getting late. Getting up from Akash's lap, she adjusted her dress. Her hair had come loose in the impromptu makeout session, and while tying it, she came forward and gave a small peck on Akash's neck. Akash again untied her hair and they walked towards the car.

'You look more beautiful with you hair open,' Akash said holding her hand lovingly.

'And you look hotter when you smile. They highlight your cute dimples,' Aleesha replied and they started their journey back home.

Romance is the language of love. It is the way you show your partner that you care about them. The time she spent with Akash had made her feel much better and she was now relaxed about moving to the hostel.

While driving back home after dropping off Aleesha, Akash sent a message to her.

The day you came into my life, everything changed. Your arrival brought with it happiness, hope, and contentment. I was afraid to give you my heart, as I was scared that you would tear it apart. Then I gradually let it commit the perfect crime because you stole my heart with no intentions of giving it back. I promise to love you in every way that I can and to be by your side in every possible way. Your beauty overwhelms me as I wrap my arms around you. I press you tight and great passion fills my inner being. The touch of your lips makes me numb. Your Mickey is on the dashboard and smiling. You are my cutest Minnie. I love you so much. Just try not to dress as beautifully as today. You may cause accidents on the road because the whole city will be gazing at you. Love you so much. Muaahh!

Aleesha read the message and replied:

Akash, are you driving or messaging? How many times have I told you not to use your cell phone while driving! Still you don't listen to me. Anyway, you know what? I can't stop talking to my friends in Kolkata about you. I love the child in you—so innocent and sweet. The mischief in your eyes and the blush upon your cheeks, makes your dimples look very cute. The tender way you spoke today showed me that you care. Your warm hand that gently touched my hair gave me a sensation of your true love. When I first met you, I liked you but we were supposed to be friends. Who would have thought that I would love you till the end? I love the way you tell me that I am beautiful and the way you make me laugh like no one else. I love the way you move my hair away from my eyes and then kiss me on my face. It feels like I am dreaming. You too are my cutest Mickey. Love you Akash! Be mine forever. Never go away. ☺ I will remember July 20 as the day we spent our first passionate evening together. That too in public:P

Aleesha was content that Akash had no issues with her shifting to the college hostel. It was love all the way! At least for now.

In a couple of days, Aleesha finished all the hostel formalities and paperwork. The girls' hostel was not in the college campus but located at some distance from it. She had taken a double sharing room along with her classmate Kritika. According to hostel rules, girls had to compulsorily report for a roll call at 8:15 pm. One late pass was allowed in a week and one stayover per month. Girls on a late pass had to report at 10:15 pm.

Kritika, though born and brought up in Mumbai, preferred staying in the hostel as her home was located on the outskirts of Mumbai and travelling daily to college was time and energy consuming. She was Aleesha's classmate and they both had decided to take a twin sharing room. She was a bubbly girl with short hair and cute looks. Indeed she was the girl next door. She carried immense positive energy that could make anyone feel happy. According to her, the reason behind her charm and beauty was the crystal she carried with her at all times. She wore a locket around her neck which had an amethyst crystal. She believed that it was a symbol of positive energy and could seduce anyone around her. Kritika was extremely friendly and used to gel very well with everyone. Her friendly behaviour had already made her good friends with Aleesha. They were also together in their project group and thus sharing the room was like a cherry on the cake.

Aleesha decided to shift on the same day as she had finished all the formalities and Kritika too had shifted a day before. She came back to her apartment from college at around 12 pm and saw Tamanna in the kitchen preparing food. Tamanna had come home early to help Aleesha pack her bags and bid her goodbye. Aleesha felt good, as such a gesture was least expected from Tamanna. She never tried to interfere in Aleesha's personal life apart from a few nightouts that they had gone on together.

After packing up, Aleesha look around the place one last time to check if she had left something. She was about to leave when Tamanna hugged her and said:

'Keep in touch. In case you face any problems, feel free to seek my help. I'm not that far from your college. Also if you feel like returning to this apartment, then you are most welcome.'

'Thanks Tammy di,' Aleesha smiled and continued, 'When are you shifting?'

'Most probably tomorrow.'

Taking the bags out of the lift, Tamanna accompanied Aleesha to the cab. Aleesha gave a last look at the apartment after which the taxi sped off to her new place.

'Kritika, have you prepared the slides for the presentation?' asked Aleesha, unpacking her bag. Kritika was busy working on something on her laptop.

The rooms were not as bad as Aleesha had thought. First year students were allocated rooms on the ground floor of the hostel building. There was a long corridor with a series of rooms one after the other in a row. Aleesha's room had two single beds with an attached washroom. Apart from the wooden beds with cotton mattresses and pillows, each girl was given a small steel almirah to keep their belongings and a small dressing table. The wall above the bed was plastered with posters of latest film stars, probably put up by the room's previous occupants. What Aleesha liked the most about the room was that it had an AC and a small balcony as well. There was a canteen situated on the ground floor itself and had fixed meal timings. Still Kritika had bought with her a packet of chips which she was munching on while browsing the internet on her laptop.

'I am searching for some hot photos of Robert Pattinson. I wish I could find a nude one. I would take off these posters on the wall and put up just his picture,' Kritika said with a naughty smile on her face.

'Ya, he is fucking hot. I have watched his intimate scene from *Twilight* so many times and I still feel goosebumps every time I watch it,' Aleesha replied.

'Are you engaged? I mean are you dating someone?' Kritika asked casually. She was a complete mismatch to Tamanna. Kritika liked getting involved in the personal affairs of other people, not because she loved gossiping, but because she was overfriendly.

'Yes. His name is Akash. He is working at the RS Group here in Mumbai itself. We met sometime back in a club,' Aleesha answered.

'I am sure he is not as hot as Robert. Look at this pic. I could literally bite his lips. They are so juicy,' Kritika exclaimed.

They both laughed and together downloaded some hot pictures of their favourite stars. Aleesha was tired from all the unpacking and fell on the bed, tired. They both had a long chat about their past, family, friends, boyfriends, and fantasies.

It was Aleesha's first day in the hostel and she was gelling well with Kritika. Aleesha had already started making plans of breaking the hostel rules and bringing Akash in her room at least during nighttime. Even Kritika gave her the green signal. After some time they switched off the lights of the room and covered themselves with a blanket.

'You are a darling. Love you sweetie,' Aleesha told Kritika for being such a sport and letting Akash come at night.

'Go to sleep baby. It's too late. Presentations and exams are just round the corner,' Kritika said jokingly to which both of them laughed.

Aleesha sent a message to Akash before closing her eyes.

Good night Mickey. Your Minnie is tired and needs to sleep badly. Miss you a lot. Muaahhh. Love you.

Exploring the 'No-Male' Territory

'You are out of your mind!' I uttered.

'I am serious dude. Aleesha and her friend Kritika have planned it all out. We just need to act like it's a scripted show. So chill,' Akash said trying to convince me. To some extent, he was succeeding too.

I was still lost in thought and didn't understand the gravity of the situation until Akash repeated those words. 'Girls' Hostel'. I woke up from my dream as if someone had given me an electric shock.

'Crazy? You will be fucked and you will screw her life too if we get caught. Have you lost it?' I shouted getting up from my seat.

'It will be full on dhamaal. There will be just girls and more girls. The whole attention will be on us,' Akash rejoiced. Then looking at my expressionless face, he continued, 'Aadi, calm down. We will take extra care so that no one can catch us and the girls will anyway be there to guide us. So relax.'

The debate continued for almost an hour and finally I gave up. I agreed to tag along even after knowing the risks involved. One of the deciding factors was that I felt Aleesha was smart enough to handle such things. She had done it brilliantly during the party. The only thing I wished was that Akash would not mess it up like last time.

Akash messaged Aleesha who was busy with studies and preparations for the approaching presentation.

Aditya has agreed. You look in to the rest of the things carefully. Let's have fun this Saturday. I won't disturb you much until then. All the best for your presentation tomorrow. Love you.

Aleesha read the message twice and replied with a kiss smiley. She was tensed about the presentation because even Kritika hadn't prepared for it yet.

'We hardly have any time left. Let's prepare some basic slides and Google the rest of the content. We need to be spontaneous tomorrow,' Aleesha said looking worried while Kritika started jotting down the points.

'I think we will do well. We hardly need to speak for ten minutes. Quite manageable,' Kritika assured her opening her book to look for further information on the topic.

'Darling, we have not been told to talk about our boyfriends or crushes that we can go on speaking for hours,' Aleesha joked. 'Even then I wonder if I would be able to speak for more than fifteen minutes.'

'Why not? You just need to talk about Akash and your relationship. If it's worth listening to, then I will record it too so that I can make him listen to it. He will go crazy hearing you talk about him,' Kritika laughed.

Realizing they had very little time left before the exam, they became serious and in the next couple of hours, their entire presentation was ready. Both of them had not only prepared the slides but also studied a bit for the coming examination. It was around 1 am and both of them were feeling really hungry. Kritika had chips and dry fruits with her. They were busy gorging on chips when Aleesha's mobile beeped. It was Akash. Kritika couldn't stop herself from asking out of curiosity,

'What important thing does he have to tell you just before going to sleep?'

Aleesha couldn't stop smiling. The message read: `I want to tell you that your dressing style needs a makeover. I know exactly what will look good on you... and that's me. Try it!`

She read the message aloud for Kritika and they both started giggling. They decided to play a prank on him. Kritika took her cell phone and said, 'That's called phone swap. Your poor boyfriend. Now let me continue the chat. I hope you don't mind,' she winked and sent Akash a message.

`Your size will be too small for me. My friend says I need one size bigger. What do you think?`

Both of them were enjoying this act and waited anxiously for Akash's reply. Within a few seconds, a message popped up on the screen.

`You don't need one, Minnie. I am there to cover you.`

Kritika was in no mood to stop. She sent another one:

`I prefer to be without cover, my Mickey. But I am not your Minnie. :P`

Akash must have been in a state of shock after the message as he called up Aleesha a couple of times after that.

`What do you mean?` he replied.

`I mean, I am not Aleesha. I am Kritika. :D :D`

They waited for some more time for him to reply after the secret was out, but Akash didn't. Aleesha called him up a couple of times as well but he didn't pick up his phone.

Kritika couldn't stop laughing. She was busy browsing through a magazine.

'What are you reading?' Aleesha asked.

'Dumb ass, it's *Cosmopolitan* magazine. Only for girls,' Kritika answered closing her laptop.

'Oh is it? I have heard about it but have never read it. Show it to me too.' Aleesha couldn't hide her excitement.

'Wait, I will read it out for you,' Kritika said, picking out an article. 'There is a column in this edition titled, "30 Things To Do With a Naked Man." Another one says...'

Aleesha interrupted her before she could read any further. 'Does this magazine really have such kind of things written in it? I had thought that my friends used to lie on BBM when they talked about reading such articles in magazines'

'Try reading this one. It's quite an eye opener,' Kritika said and handed over the magazine to Aleesha.

Once Aleesha began reading it, there was no stopping her.

'You are taking so much of interest in the article, almost as if you are going to apply them on Akash. He might get lucky someday then,' Kritika teased.

'Shut up. He is better than me and knows how to handle such situations,' Aleesha said in a naughty tone.

'Is it? Do tell me your stories. It will be fun. You know what happened when I was in a relationship? It's been almost a year now. When I made love to my boyfriend for the first time, the experience was not so great. He called me up the next day to ask me if I had told my best friend about it. I told him, "Of course!" Needless to say, he made a greater effort the next time we made out.'

Aleesha couldn't control her laughter and almost banged her head against the wall. It was too much for her to bear.

After all the girl talk, they both fell asleep. Aleesha and Kritika had been gelling very well together and had started discussing their personal problems with each other too. This in turn benefitted their college presentations due to their understanding and coordination. They were like two volumes of one book. Best friends often come into your life at the most perfect times and Aleesha had found one in Kritika. Unlike other girls, they had no jealousy against each other.

The morning alarm woke Aleesha up and she did not waste her time in curling on the bed again. In the meanwhile, Kritika was wide awake and going through the presentation slides. They went to the canteen to have their breakfast and then started for college.

'Which is the first lecture?' Kritika asked taking a seat on the last bench.

'Effective Communication Skills. I hate this subject. The professor also is a super bore. He looks like Kallu mama,' Aleesha laughed resting her head on the bench.

The professor entered and the class went silent for a moment. He was wearing spectacles and had a pot belly. Aleesha felt that the yellow shirt that he had worn made him look like *Rangeela's* Aamir Khan. Both girls continued to make fun of him sitting on the last bench.

'I hope you all remember that today we are going to do an assignment on English writing. I'll give you 20 minutes to write and you will then have to randomly select someone to read it out,' he said passing the attendance sheet to the students.

Kritika was sitting next to Aleesha and was playing Angry Birds on her mobile.

'Guess what? If couples in love are called 'Love Birds', I bet a couple who've fought with each other are called "Angry Birds"' Aleesha laughed while she watched Kritika play the game.

Aleesha noticed a girl sitting ahead of them. Looking at how she was dressed, she couldn't stop herself from commenting.

'Look at that girl. What a wardrobe disaster! Who wears tube tops with embroidery on it and that too in parrot green colour? Blue denims and dark green heels. Err…Plus look at her hairstyle. Oh god!' Aleesha whispered in Kritika's ears.

'She looks like she has landed here from another planet Look at her earrings. Who wears danglers to college? A red lipstick is an add-on to the disaster. I don't think she realizes she looks like a parrot,' Kritika added.

They continued to make fun of her, least interested in what the professor was saying. And so were the other students. Aleesha looked at her mobile to check the notifications.

Akash had messaged her.

`Meet me in the evening. Let's discuss about Saturday.`

Aleesha immediately replied saying she had a class in the evening and won't be able to make it.

Akash messaged her again.

`Please come. Just for some time. Get down at Dadar station. Will meet you under the bridge.`

Aleesha thought about it for a moment. Dadar was feasible for both of them as it was the only railway station common to both the Central and Western Railway lines. It is the most crowded railway station but they had no option as Aleesha had to leave early for a class.

Akash reached the station before time and looked for Aleesha but she was nowhere to be seen. He called her and informed that he was waiting under the bridge. Hardly a few minutes later, Aleesha reached there. As Akash saw her approaching, he moved forward and hugged her for the longest time without caring about the thousands of people around them.

'Let's go to this restaurant *Rishi*. It's nearby and we can leave within an hour too,' Akash suggested. Aleesha agreed.

Once seated at the corner table in the restaurant, they started discussing about Saturday. Though Aleesha was confident about the plan, Akash was still not very confident about it. But he didn't let it show. Somewhere he felt that it could put Aleesha in trouble. She explained to him every little detail but Akash hesitated. However, a cute kiss on his cheeks and a hug elevated his confidence. Aleesha knew how to convince Akash and she did exactly the same. They moved out of the restaurant after paying the bill.

While walking back towards the railway station, Akash saw an exclusive women's shop. He kept staring at the poster inside the shop. It had a supermodel wearing a bikini on it. Aleesha didn't notice it until she turned her face towards Akash and saw him staring at the poster.

'How cheap. You're sick Akash. We're in the middle of the road and you're staring at that poster like a despo. Don't talk to me. Buzz off,' Aleesha shouted in anger and started walking ahead of Akash as if she didn't know him.

'Don't get angry jaan, please. You are my Minnie. I was not looking at her. I was thinking about something,' said Akash trying to explain himself.

'Akash stop saying jaan and Minnie and blah blah. It's not going to affect me. I can't believe the way you were staring at her cleavage. It makes me think you're with me out of desperation!'

'Oh jaan, now where are you taking this topic? I was not staring at her cleavage. Trust me. Why you are getting so hyperactive? And even if I was looking, then what's the big deal? It was just a poster. She was not real.' Akash was trying hard to convince her.

'So if she was real, you would have fucked her in the showroom itself?' Aleesha added and this increased her temper even more.

Aleesha reached the platform but Akash kept on following her. Aleesha hardly paid attention to his words.

'Akash, please leave. I will talk to you later. Please don't bug me right now. You are irritating me. Stop creating a scene here.'

'Minnie what did I do? You are not even listening to what I am saying. At least listen to me. Please. Ok please forgive me. Don't get angry. I love you jaan,' Akash almost pleaded this time.

A five seconds stare at the poster had culminated into a big fight between Akash and Aleesha. According to her, it was not about looking at the poster, it was about the way Akash was staring at the poster when Aleesha was standing right beside him. It was as if Akash had never seen a girl in a bra. It was the height of desperation.

They continued arguing for some time. Soon the train arrived. Aleesha was still firm in her decision and didn't even look at Akash. As the train halted, Aleesha boarded the ladies compartment and stood near the door. Akash was standing on the platform requesting Aleesha to get down and end the fight. All the people around them were watching them as if there a movie shoot was going on. The train started moving and Akash was still convincing her to forgive him.

'Jaan I am sorry. I won't do it again. Don't go like this, please.'

The train picked up pace and Akash got into the compartment without paying heed to the fact that it was the ladies compartment. All he could see was Aleesha's angry face and he couldn't take it. He wanted a smile from his love.

Without thinking of the consequences, he jumped in the compartment in the running train. As it was late afternoon, the train towards CST was not as crowded as during peak hours. Some of the ladies gave strange expressions and some even passed lewd comments. Akash pulled both his ears to apologize like a kid. Aleesha was hurt deep inside by Akash's behaviour and the argument later on increased her temper even more. Throughout the journey, they argued with each other and Akash finally gave up after reaching CST station.

'Akash, leave me alone. I'll ping you on BBM when I feel like it. Currently I am not in a mood to talk with you. Don't irritate me anymore. I beg of you,' Aleesha said rudely and walked away.

Akash stood there numb, watching Aleesha go away from him. They say if you truly love something, you should let it go. If it comes back to you, it was yours and if it doesn't, then it was never yours. But what if it doesn't come back? Though it was not as serious as Akash made it out to be, something like this had never happened with him before. Aleesha had never reacted so fiercely to anything before, and Akash was completely clueless about what should be done next. After waiting for some time, he boarded the train and sat alone at the window seat listening to songs on his iPod.

He looked outside the window to see everything slowly fade in the darkness. Fights do happen, but when you are not used to them, they hurt. This is somewhat similar to academics. Students do fail, but when you fail for the first time, it hurts. Then you get used to the process of failing.

Akash reached home and messaged me.

This is the problem when you are attached to someone. When they leave, you just feel lost.

I was half-asleep and could hardly read his message. I didn't take it seriously too. Even he was about to sleep when his phone beeped. He expected it to be me but it was Aleesha.

I am sorry. I know I overreacted to the whole thing, but even you were wrong. You should have thought before saying those words which hurt me. I shouldn't have been so rude but I lost it. I promise I will never fight again. Please forget my harsh words and come out of your dark mood. Show me your lovely smile and let me kiss your dimples. It's said forgiveness in a relationship is essential. I realize my mistake now, but at that time, I couldn't stand seeing you looking at someone else with so much desperation. Am I not hot? I have better ones. :D. Sorry. You know, the thing that I realized after our first fight is that I know our relationship can survive a disagreement too. I cried when I left the station. I know you were hurt and it was killing me from inside. I couldn't cheer up knowing that there were tears in your eyes. The lips with a drop of tear on it are the best ones to kiss. Let me kiss you. Muahhhhh! Love you Mickey... I am eagerly waiting for Saturday.

Akash immediately called her up and her kisses seemed more beautiful on the phone after a fight. Her voice seemed more melodious than ever. Aleesha not only cared for him, but also felt protective towards him. Akash felt Aleesha was the best girl he could ever get. After a long conversation, Aleesha hung up the phone. When you are talking to someone special, even a nonsensical conversation makes sense. Akash had realized it that day. He changed his BBM status to,

`Aaja dil ki kare saude baazi kya narazi... Aa re aa re aa re aa! Waiting for Saturday!`

Aleesha copied the same status with a dance smiley.

My cell phone beeped. It was Akash again.

`I really cannot understand girls. Some time back she was on the verge of killing me and now she is in love with me all over again. Girls I tell you!`

As I saw the sender's name, I replied without even reading the full message:

`Arre, go to sleep yaar. Let me sleep too.`

Saturday finally arrived. Akash and I were excited and nervous at the same time. Breaking the rules of a girls' hostel and sneaking in could be nasty if we were caught.

'If you get caught then you at least have a valid reason. You can tell them that you're Aleesha's boyfriend. What can I say? That I'm a tharki who just came for sightseeing? Like tours and travels take you to Mumbai Darshan, Akash took me to Girls Darshan?' I yelled.

'Keep your mouth shut, Aadi. You're speaking shit. Don't worry, nothing's going to happen,' Akash assured me.

This was the first time I was doing such a bold thing. I had not even during my college days. And now because of tried anything like this Akash, even I had been dragged into it. I was nervous as hell.

'I wish I had listened to my mom,' I said nervously.

'What did she say?' Akash asked while dialling Aleesha's number on his cell.

'When I have not even called her up, how can I possibly tell you?' I criticized.

We were standing in a dark passage near the girl's hostel which was hidden from public view. Aleesha told him over the phone that the warden was not around, so it was the perfect chance for us to slip into the hostel. Akash didn't think much about the consequences because getting into a girls' hostel was quite thrilling. It was no different for me but my nervousness overshadowed the thrill.

We were almost ready to walk towards the main gate when Aleesha messaged Akash.

Akash, just wait for some time. I just checked the building and saw that the workers in the dining hall are still there. But the warden won't return so soon. So let the workers move out and you guys can slip in after they leave.

'Crazy, what if we would have...?' I panicked.

'Chill.' Akash took out a pack of cigarettes, handed one to me, and said, 'Smoke one. You will feel better. Don't eat my head now.'

I lit a cigarette and slowly inhaled a puff. No one was around. We were at the corner of the road, some away 200 metres from the main gate.

'Akash, I am going to lead the way. You follow me. It's not because I have suddenly got some energy after smoking but because I don't trust you on this anymore,' I whispered.

As we got the confirmation from Aleesha, we quickly changed into dark T-shirts to avoid unnecessary attention. We walked ahead and waited near the tree which was not far from the main gate. An evil smile emerged on Akash's. My nervousness had taken a back seat face and the momentary situation had increased my excitement. We climbed the wall which acted as a barrier between us and the girls' dormitory.

'It's time to explore the "no male territory",' Akash whispered in my ear.

I gave Akash a wicked smile and got inside as quietly as possible. Our eyes scanned all the passageways and we stealthily headed towards Aleesha's room. The door was kept slightly open and the lights were switched off. We heard some noise from the left corridor and we both stared at each other without moving our feet. We stood standstill, scared. I signalled for him to run and get inside the room as quickly he could since we were hardly a few metres away from the source of the noise. Akash pushed the door open and I followed him inside. When we got inside, Akash closed the door behind us. Aleesha quickly latched the door and switched on the lights. Akash and Aleesha hugged each other tightly in excitement. They had executed the plan successfully.

'So we finally made it,' Kritika cheered.

Aleesha introduced us to Kritika. We greeted each other formally and then sat comfortably on the bed after keeping our bags in one corner.

'I hope no one saw us coming,' I said, still a bit shaken up from the experience.

'I don't think so. Else, there would have been total chaos outside. The administration is a bit strict here. However, we are not the only ones who break rules. There are lots of seniors who don't follow any timings,' Aleesha said giving us a glass of water.

We hardly cared now as we were already inside. After a little chitchat with Aleesha and Kritika, I opened my bag which had all the fun stuff. Kritika's face was so delighted when I opened my Sheesha kit that she almost jumped from her bed.

'Double apple,' both the girls shouted at the same time.

I took out two pipes from the bag. Aleesha immediately took one while I asked Akash to clear the other pipe by blowing air into it. I had planned to smoke hookah while we all chatted and got to know each other. Hookah smoking promotes a social atmosphere and people can sip the hookah while getting to know each other.

'Kritika, I heard you fooled Akash by sending messages through Aleesha's cell phone, pretending to be her? I wish I could see his reaction.' I said giving Akash a naughty look.

Everyone started laughing, including Aleesha. She pulled his cheeks with love and then gave him a slight peck on his lips.

'Ahem Ahem! Someone really cares,' Kritika teased him and I joined her in teasing them.

Akash and Aleesha sat in one corner of the room to get some privacy while Kritika and I were still feasting on the hookah. It was almost early morning and we didn't even realize how time passed by. Kritika and I had a long chat while puffing the hookah. I remembered that I had something special in my bag.

'I present to you a special dish prepared by the man himself. Mr Akash,' I said in a rhythmic tone.

Aleesha and Kritika were stunned after hearing this. I started laughing and told them that Akash was a really good cook. Akash in the meanwhile kept mum, smiling all the while. He indeed was a good cook which made him a hot favourite among the girls.

'Wow. Aleesha, you are super lucky. I wish I could get someone like him who would cook for me whenever I am tired or don't feel like cooking. That's so cute of him,' Kritika said patting Akash's back.

'Aditya, have you ever done anything like this ever before?' Aleesha asked me.

'Errr… I don't know how to cook at all. The only food items I can cook are Maggi and omelette. I can even make tea,' I said biting my tongue between my teeth.

'Then you are not my type. Leave. I will have to search for a better option,' said Kritika joining in the conversation.

'Go ahead. Who is stopping you?' I said teasingly in my don't-care-a-damn attitude.

Aleesha fell head over heels in love with Akash as he had whipped up a wonderful dish for her. He had made pasta for everyone. The way he cared for Aleesha and expressed his love was something very unique. He knew Aleesha liked pasta and thus he had spent the entire evening making her favourite dish.

'I made it just for you, my Minnie. I love you and I am yours forever,' said Akash.

'I think even I should learn how to cook to impress girls,' I winked.

'Aditya, you don't have to be a great chef to make great food. The effort you put in to make something as simple as Maggi in the kitchen is what really matters. Moreover, even if it turns out to be average in taste, the fact that you tried is what is admirable,' Aleesha explained.

'I would personally prefer a boyfriend who cooks a decent meal for me rather than one who spends a lot of money to take me out. I think it's very cute when a boy takes out time and has that much patience to cook a meal for his girlfriend. I find it really sweet!' Kritika added.

Akash's efforts made Aleesha go crazy for him and she couldn't resist kissing him. She almost had the urge to push him against the wall and kiss him passionately.

'If you guys are done eating, can we get to taste the pasta as well?' I interrupted them. Aleesha blushed and covered her face with her hands.

Aleesha and Akash were two such souls whose union defined true love. Akash was feeding Aleesha the pasta with his own hands.

After eating, we decided to move out of the hostel before anyone got up. We packed our bags and waited for Aleesha's next instruction. She took a bottle of water and after switching off the lights, opened the door slightly. She told us to wait inside without uttering a word. She went near the cooler and while filling the bottle, looked around to see if anyone was awake. There was not a single soul to be seen, and once she assured herself, she came back to inform us. We took our bags and stepped outside the door. I steathily moved my feet towards the gate.

I turned back to warn Akash to hurry up and saw him kissing Aleesha at the doorstep. I wanted to shout at him out of irritation. We had already broken the rules and instead of moving out as soon as possible, there he was busy kissing her! I walked towards him and forcefully pulled him by the collar. We saw someone on the first floor flicking on the light, so we ran outside as quickly as possible.

Akash waved goodbye to Aleesha before climbing out through the wall. We had safely crossed the hurdle and were now on the main road. I immediately removed a pack of cigarettes and smoked a puff to ease my tension. The night had been no less than an adventure for us. But we had all enjoyed the thrill of it. We were glad to be in each other's company. After all, some form of craziness is needed to keep the thrill alive in your life. Otherwise, life gets boring.

Corporate Atyachaar

'Hey Deep, come join us. I just read somewhere that sleeping during work hours is acceptable in Japan,' shouted one of the employees seeing Deep entering the cafeteria.

'Are you serious?' Deep laughed, pulling out a chair.

'Ya. It's viewed as exhaustion from working hard, though some people fake it to look committed to their job. I wonder when Indian corporate houses will understand this.'

Everyone laughed while Deep's eyes searched for Tamanna. She could not be seen anywhere.

It had been almost two weeks, but the post-party incident was still fresh in Deep's mind. From that day, he pretended as if nothing happened. Even Tamanna didn't remember what she had said or how she had behaved. Though everything seemed to be normal on the surface, the truth was that only Deep knew that things were not in place. He had to seal his lips for he wanted an appraisal. Within a couple of months, a 'performance appraisal' was to be held and he didn't want to spoil his image in front of others. Thus, he simply ignored it.

'Try to answer this question. Tell me three signs that show a person is working in the corporate world,' one of them asked jokingly.

Deep thought for a moment and smiled.

'Stressed, depressed, and still well dressed.'

Everyone looked at each other and burst out in laughter. It was hilarious. This time it was Deep's turn.

'Guys, can you tell me what is recession?'

'When "water and wife" replace "wine and women".'

Their humorous session continued for a bit. Just as they were about to disperse, Tamanna entered the cafeteria and told them to move towards the hall. She also told them that the selection of candidates for the Goa project conference would be done after the training session that was to be held in the hall.

'Deep,' Tamanna called after him as she spotted him.

Deep looked back at her with a raised eyebrow. Tamanna covered the gap separating them and started walking beside him.

'I have recommended your name for the appraisal along with a couple of other names,' she winked. She was much more comfortable with Deep after the party since she didn't remember anything about the incident.

He simply nodded at her without any expression on his face. Situations like these embarrassed him every time but all he could do was kick his own ass. Once inside the hall, he took his seat alongside the entire team while Tamanna stood beside them. All the managers were made to stand for reasons unknown to them.

Tamanna kept glancing towards Deep at regular intervals.

After some time, the trainer entered the room and, adjusting his collar mic, came and stood at the center of the stage. He greeted everyone and started with his speech. He was humorous, which was evident when he made a pretty girl stand up and said to her, 'Let me Kiss.'

She was shocked to hear it. However, within a few seconds he laughed and said, 'I mean 'Let me Keep It Short and Simple. My name is Arun Bhattacharya.'

'Can you tell me why I have made all the managers stand? Especially the women? Let me share with you one incident which occured in my office. The lady manager had to report to the head of the department. When she entered his cabin, he asked her, "Are you free tonight?" She immediately smiled and said yes. The next moment, that rascal gave her a hundred sheets to type out. Now you all might be thinking who the actual rascal was. Whoever it was, I don't care... The lesson to learn from the example I just told you is the importance of ethics.'

As he continued talking, Tamanna glanced at Deep and smiled. The training continued for almost a couple of hours during which Mr Arun shared the product details and many more valuable experiences. He was about to end the session with a final note.

'Before leaving, I would like to tell you about the circle of life. Many of you might be Engineers or MBA graduates but in your practical life, the sooner you understand the difference between your college and office life, the better it will be for you. The sooner you adapt to the changes, the faster you will excel in life. In college, we had different professors assigned for different subjects, but here we have only one task and only one manager. Your task is to improve your performance. In college, you bunked your lectures and spent money whereas here if you bunk, you lose money. In college, you were at least aware about your exam dates, but here can anyone tell clearly about the audit dates?'

Everyone laughed as he carried on with his speech. He paused for a moment to drink water and continued:

'If you score less marks in an examination but still manage to clear it, you need not be answerable to anyone. But here if you score less, which means if your performance goes down, then you are answerable to all your higher authorities. Why? Because in college you paid the fees and here, you are getting paid for your work. The most important difference is that during your college days your girlfriend was proud about your clothes but now she would only feel proud if you are paid heavy salaries. Thus my dear, you better adapt yourself accordingly. You should always remember "To improve is to change but to be perfect is to change often".'

The training session was over but Deep still hadn't moved from his seat. He was continuously thinking about the motivational part of the training session and felt it was good only for training sessions. He felt so because whenever he tried to apply those concepts in real, he failed. Tamanna waited for the others to move out from the hall.

'Bullshit! All this is crap. What the fuck does he mean by "adapt yourself" '. Is it practically possible? That bloody slut whom he asked to stand sleeps almost every day with her manager. She is being paid for all the leaves and she has no other responsibilities apart from sucking his dick. Those scoundrels even make out in office premises. I mean, how cheap is that! And this Arun talks about ethics and adaptability! We work like dogs and still get no returns unless there are a few who lose everything for success. Is success more important than happiness? Cut the crap! Until the time we realize what success is and what is happiness, it's too late. Get up in the morning and catch the bus to reach the office and if you miss that bus then you lose your one-day salary. Now was I driving the bus? And if these people are so obsessed with the timings then why don't they provide pick and drop transport facilities to their employees? When you come home in the evening with your brains fucked up because of the work pressure and are just on the verge of taking a breather, you get a call from your manager asking you why you didn't raise the ticket for completing the project and submitting the work report. So was I fucking your wife the entire day in office? What was I doing on that bloody seventeen-inch computer screen? Do you even allow us to access Facebook so that I can chat with some hot chicks? No. But who will understand our problem? Moreover, the bumper prize comes ahead of this. If you are excellent in all the aspects of your work, then you are given a branded laptop with the latest configuration. You fly on cloud nine for all the appreciation you have got and try to watch some movie in the night on the same bloody laptop. Then your mobile beeps and you are ordered to come online to resolve an issue which has been suddenly raised by the authorities. Then you feel like throwing the laptop from the top floor of your building and even if you do that, you won't be satisfied. Because your BlackBerry service is still active. Therefore, in one line why don't these people just say, "You are our sex toy. We will use you as our vibrator until we derive pleasure in earning profits from you. Once we learn that you are of no use and you are not giving us the pleasure we need, we will kick you or throw you in a dustbin as we throw a condom in dustbin after sex." Moreover, all our time and energy of last few years is wasted exactly as the sperms are wasted in the condom. But ya, your virginity is lost. You are no longer a first timer. Why? Because they hand over an experience certificate saying, you are officially fucked and now you are experienced on paper. You take that and move to someone else and history once again repeats itself…'

The entire team was shocked. Their jaws had dropped down after listening to such a long speech from Deep. They just stared at him with their eyes wide open.

'He deserves to be applauded. Clap everyone,' a few employees shouted in chorus.

Deep scratched his head thinking about what he had just said. He was not even drunk. It was his frustration which he had controlled inside the hall when Mr Arun was sharing his valuable philosophies with him.

'I wish Tamanna was here. She would have enjoyed the speech so much. Can you repeat it once more please? At least we can record it,' his teammates teased him.

Tamanna joined them after some time to make the official announcement of the Goa conference.

'Ok guys, now it's time to announce the names for the Goa conference to be held in January. Managers of two teams are going to Goa for the official conference along with one employee from their team. Therefore, the authorities have shortlisted the names as per your performance. From our team, Deep will join me for the conference and from Mr Verma's team, Kajal will join us. Is that clear?' asked Tamanna.

Listening to his own name didn't surprise Deep. He had expected it right since he encountered Tamanna before the training session.

He was confused about the trip and changed the topic, saying, 'Isn't this Kajal the same girl who was with Verma?' Deep asked and everyone replied 'yes' in chorus.

'She would have really made a lot of effort last night.' The gossipmongers had begun and Deep preferred to leave the discussion before things got out of control.

Tamanna was a bit surprised as Deep had left all of a sudden without even discussing about the conference with her. She tried calling him but his cell was switched off. But that didn't trouble her since she knew Deep had to join her for the Goa conference. Missing on such an opportunity was like kicking one's luck. She was delighted to have got an opportunity to stay with Deep in Goa and didn't mind even if it was for official reasons. She had already started imagining being on Goa beaches with Deep during their free time together.

Inside her cabin, she started writing her thoughts on her Galaxy Tab.

I can't help but think that somewhere inside of you, I exist. Somewhere between liking me, loving me, and everything in the middle, you get scared. The tingling feeling terrifies you and you don't know in which direction to go.

Call me crazy, but I think I mean something to you even though you hide your real feelings. Call me weird, but I don't think you can run away from these feelings forever. I think you are eventually going to accept the fact that I make your world go round.

Was this her obsession or her love? She just wanted Deep to reciprocate her feelings in some form. Maybe a kiss or a hug or something more than that would heal her pain during bad times. Was it love or lust? She hardly knew and she hardly cared.

Deep on the other hand was confused about the whole situation. He had obviously made up his mind, but he did not know how to stop Tamanna from crossing her limits.

He called up his friend with whom he had discussed about Tamanna earlier.

'You know, the situation is something like I need to cross a river with water snakes in it. Now I can take a chance by swimming to the other side, as there are hopes that I will survive. However, what if I am told not to get wet? That's impossible. You know everything including the party incident. I'm confused. Please tell me what I should do.'

'Don't panic. If you need to cross a river without getting wet, use a boat. Simple! Why do you think so much? Just don't entertain anyone beyond what is expected of you. A bit here and there is okay. Just remember to concentrate on your work and your future wife. These are your priorities. Let me give you an example. You know when you're desperate to have sex…when your girlfriend texts you asking you if you want to have sex with her tonight, and you just type YES, and when you are supposed to send it; suddenly a thief snatches your cell and runs away. Instead of shouting for help, you shout "SEND MAAR!! SEND MAAR!" What I mean is forget the mobile, concentrate on your goal, your work. Chill!'

Deep remained silent for a moment and then both of them had a hearty laugh over the example. Deep disconnected the phone and took a deep breath. He was all set to Go Goa in January!

Unhooked and Booked

It was that time of the year when your social life is in complete shatters, you are stressed, busy, and on the verge of going completely mental. Only students can explain what they feel like when they hear the word 'Exam'. Aleesha and Kritika had almost stopped reading *Cosmopolitan* magazines and downloading hot photos of actors. All they downloaded now were PDF files of exam course or assignments to study for the internal exams.

'There are only two times when I sing the "tadap tadap ke" song. One, when I have a break up and the other, whenever there are exams. Who made this examination system? If I get to meet his family members, I will not hesitate to kill those scoundrels,' said Kritika.

'Seriously yaar. I am fed up. These exams have screwed our freedom. Just a few hours and we will be free. Hope you remember we are going to Aditya's place after the exam?' asked Aleesha turning the pages of the book.

It was this Economics paper and though the entire portion was not coming for the internals, Aleesha had not prepared for the examination in the excitement of it being the last paper. She was going through some important points just before entering the examination hall. However, it was too late. She hardly understood anything now. Economics is not a subject to be studied at the last minute. Aleesha tried her best to remember the points. She had kept the mini Xerox notes inside her top so that no one could touch them. She was extremely smart at such things.

'Let's get inside. There is hardly any time left,' said Kritika closing her book as she walked inside the classroom.

Aleesha went and took her seat which was in the centre of the classroom. She was happy that she had got enough cover fire to remove the chits. As the exam started and the professor got busy in paperwork, she looked at everyone and slowly removed the chits. Kritika was troubling her from behind to show whatever she had written. She sat across and kept her paper open so that Kritika could copy.

'Write fast, I need to turn the page. Should I?' Aleesha asked after making sure the professor was not observing them.

'Wait, wait. Just a minute. I am on the last line.' Kritika replied copying Aleesha's notes at bullet speed.

The bell rang after some time and the professor collected all the answer sheets. Aleesha came out in a happy mood as she had answered all the questions to the best of her ability. Kritika looked a bit confused and Aleesha asked her the reason for it.

'I did a blunder I suppose. I wrote one answer from the chit that you passed me. But I wrote it in a hurry, I didn't see what I was writing and I think I have screwed up. I also wrote the line which read "Refer to page no 181 for the third point",' Kritika remembered.

Aleesha started laughing aloud and teased Kritika for her stupidity. Kritika felt sad but Aleesha cheered her up by reminding her about their plan. Akash was going to meet them outside the college and then all three of them were going to head towards my home.

'How was your paper?' Akash questioned.

'Akash, asking this question itself is useless. Even Aamir Khan wouldn't have taken so much effort to tatoo his body and prepare chits that Aleesha takes during her exams. She is a lady Gajini,' Kritika commented after which all of them started laughing.

She was not wrong. The time Aleesha had spent in preparing chits and taking mini Xerox notes for the exam was unbelievable. She never got caught as she kept them at a place which no man could touch without permission.

Within an hour, they reached my apartment and I went down to receive them. As they entered my house, they pounced upon the glasses vodka, which I had bought especially for the girls. I was not in a mood to drink so I had just brought a Breezer for myself. Akash preferred vodka along with the girls.

'Aadi, are you sure no one is going to come home at this time?' Akash enquired.

'No. I don't think so. Dad has gone to Andheri for work and mom won't return till evening for sure.' I informed them opening my bottle of Breezer.

After a few pegs, Akash and the girls changed into more comfortable clothes. Akash wore my cotton track pants with a sleeveless T-shirt. Aleesha and Kritika had carried their clothes along with them. Aleesha wore short pants which barely covered her thighs while Kritika wore leggings. Once comfortably seated in my bedroom, we took our positions to play on the PlayStation. I sat on Akash's lap to control the remote while Kritika sat in front of Aleesha. We were playing 'Tekken' with Asuka Kazama and having a ball of a time together.

My bedroom door was exactly in front of us beside the screen. I had just latched it. While playing, we didn't hear the sound of the doorbell. So we were caught completely off guard when my dad entered my bedroom unannounced. He had a spare key to my bedroom. No one understood what to do and remained fixed to their spots like statues. I glanced at everyone and saw Kritika trying to hide her glass of vodka while Aleesha was still sitting with her glass in her hand. I was sitting on Akash's lap resting the back of my head on his chest while Akash was holding on to me with both his hands making it seem almost like an embrace. At that moment, I just wished my dad didn't feel we were upto something different looking at our positions. I behaved as cool as possible and greeted him.

'Hi dad, you are early today?'

'Ya beta. I finished my work earlier than expected. So what's happening?' he asked trying to sound casual.

'Nothing. We were playing games and just chilling out,' I replied moving out of my bedroom and walking towards the kitchen to bring him a glass of water. He followed me into the kitchen.

'Do you have any problem, beta? I mean there is nothing wrong with you, right? Who are they and what's happening?' dad said sounding confused.

'Chill dad, we are just friends. I am sorry for the drinks. Trust me, I don't drink. They wanted to have some vodka so they got it. Their exams have just got over. The girl who was sitting on the lap of the other girl is Aleesha. She is Akash's girlfriend. The other one is Kritika,' I explained to him.

'You were not doing something else, right? You and Akash?'

'Oh dad, it's nothing like that. I am straight. Akash is just a friend and we were playing games so were caught in that position,' I replied casually.

Holy crap, he must have thought Ma da Laadla bigad gaya. I had never in my wildest dreams thought he would think something like that about me. I wished Akash had sat on Aleesha's lap. At least that would have not put me in an embarrassing spot. He kept on staring at me.

'Dad, trust me,' I said in a convincing tone.

'The world today is full of homosexual couples, so I thought of asking you directly. Don't be shy if you are hiding something. Be clear. Yesterday even your mom was asking me why you always close your door when you are sitting in your bedroom. She couldn't ask you, but tell me frankly—do you watch adult films after closing the door? It's okay if you are. It's normal at this age,' he said keeping his plate in the dishwasher.

'Dad, why would I close the door to watch such things? These things can no longer be viewed only on the computer. You can easily watch them on your mobile phone. But don't worry. I am not doing anything wrong,' I said trying to make him understand there was nothing serious.

'If you are not doing anything wrong, then why do you close the door?' he asked.

He was not wrong from his point of view. He gave me a typical dad's lecture for around 15 minutes and left after that. I closed the door and came back to my room. Everyone was anxious to know dad's reaction. I told them the entire story of what he thought about Akash and me. We all rolled on the floor laughing.

After playing for some time, we had some snacks and then watched a movie on my computer. Akash came to me and whispered in my ear that he wanted to stay alone with Aleesha for some time. I told him that he could go to the master bedroom and close the door.

'Akash, but do lock the door or dad might come again and catch you in an embarrassing situation,' I teased him.

Aleesha pinched my arms and tried to slap me. Akash caught Aleesha while we were running all over the house and hugged her tight. She lifted her toes gently and kissed his eyes. He took her to the other room while Kritika and I relaxed on the bed watching a movie.

'Akash, take it easy. I want you to be gentle,' Aleesha whispered when Akash tried to push her towards the wall and kiss her.

'My Minnie wants me to be gentle today. Aww. I will be as gentle as possible my baby,' Akash muttered playing with her hands against the wall.

He started off with kissing her neck. Aleesha moaned in pleasure. There were no dim lights, scented candles, or satin sheets around them, but they were experiencing lovemaking for the first time which made it all the more special.

The cold air of the AC started showing its effects on Akash. He was so close to her that he could smell her hair and her body which was so exotic. He inched closer to her and turned her face to the wall. He started rubbing her back and caressing her thighs over the hot pants that barely covered her ass. Aleesha was holding his right hand and pressing it whenever she moaned. She gave a mischievous smile and pushed Akash on the bed. She moved closer to him and started kissing him all over his body.

'Aleesha, you look so beautiful and sexy. You are one hot Minnie,' Akash teased her while sliding his hands inside her top.

'Aaahh! Slowly Mickey. I am not going anywhere. You broke my hot pant's button. Sometimes you behave like a kid who gets so excited after getting a chocolate that he tries to bite it so hard that in the process he eventually lands up biting his own tongue. But you look so seductive when you are in a romantic mood,' Aleesha whispered rolling her fingers on his chest and gently moving it downwards.

The next moment Aleesha's clothes were off. She was just in her bottoms and bra. She had worn a nice transparent bra and Akash couldn't stop himself from staring at her.

'Naughty innerwear, haan?' Akash teased her.

'Don't act like a big despo though I know you are one,' Aleesha said.

'What did you say? That I'm a despo? And the way you moaned in the living room after I touched you. What does that show? That you...' he said and hugged Aleesha tightly, kissing her bare shoulders and back.

'You look so sexy, sweetheart. Even Megan Fox cannot look as hot as you on bed. You look so delectable that if I was a man-eater, I would have eaten you up,' Akash said getting aroused.

'Aaaaahh!' Aleesha moaned as he slowly removed her bra with his teeth. She had a satisfied look on her face. At the same time she knew it was just the beginning of their long love-making session. She could see the love and passion in his eyes, something she had always dreamt of seeing in the eyes of her prince charming. She couldn't hold herself any longer and kissed him passionately. It was a long, aggressive kiss this time. Akash removed the ice cube from his glass of vodka and rolled it all over her body. She let out a loud moan tearing off Akash's clothes and reversing their positions. She put her legs across his body and allowed Akash to take charge. Her dirty talks in a sexy, mesmerizing voice, aroused him. She scratched her nails on his back like a hungry tigress. Akash searched for the condom which he had secretly slipped under the pillow when they had entered the room. He hurriedly tried to open the packet, but for some reason, it wouldn't open. Aleesha started chuckling looking at Akash.

'Poor baby. Mickey doesn't even know how to open the packet,' Aleesha teased him.

He looked crossly at Aleesha and went back to concentrating on opening the packet. He failed again. He looked here and there to find something to open it. He was lucky enough to find a pair of scissors on the side table. He finally succeeded in opening it with the scissors and Aleesha laughed out loudly, pulling his cheeks. Akash sealed her mouth by giving her a hard kiss which turned into a passionate French kiss that lasted for more than five minutes. Aleesha had reached the peak of sexual arousal and desired for more than foreplay. Finally, Akash was completely inside her and a drop of tear rolled down Aleesha's eyes. Akash moved closer and kissed the tear.

'Please, baby, don't stop. Take your strong hands and handcuff me. You're my love cop. Arrest me in your arms and make me beg for mercy. Come on baby! Take me on a romantic ride today and make this moment as steamy as never before,' Aleesha muttered biting his earlobes.

Eventually the pain dissolved and they were left with a strange and mildly pleasurable sense of conquest. It was a world of romance and they just longed for more and more. They had never known such pleasure and satisfaction. Aleesha's heart raced and her body was left trembling. She moved her hips up in the air and started to moan uncontrollably. She waited to feel the thrust of his manhood pulsating inside her repeatedly until she pleaded for him to stop. Akash moved his lips near her ears and whispered slowly. 'I love you Minnie. Be mine always.'

'My hottie Mickey, today I feel so complete, so content. Never leave me, Akash. I love you to the core.' she said and hugged him tightly.

'You are so good at lovemaking. I love you so very much,' Akash whispered in her ears and she smooched him hard.

After an hour had eloped, they reluctantly got up to get dressed. Once ready, they came out of the room with a smile. I observed both of them while they sat next to us and watched the climax of the movie. They looked content with each other. I smiled to myself, for I could feel how happy they were together. They kept on staring at each other without uttering a word.

Aleesha was chained in the flames of love and Akash was melting in the fire of passion, which was so immense that even water could not quench it. They had experienced their first taste of love.

After cleaning up the room and clearing all the bottles and packet of cigarettes, they left. I accompanied them till the autorickshaw and waved them goodbye.

Akash was the first to message after reaching home.

I never thought a night at a club party would bring love in my life. It still feels like a dream. But you were there. You were real. I pinched myself a hundred times to confirm whether it was real. And it was. You came from nowhere and became one of my strongest reasons to live. A current of emotions pulled us closer. Your flirty voice makes me go weak in the knees and your bewitching eyes provoke me to feel your skin and make love to you. When you said 'you are my love cop', I felt aroused and your dirty talks took me to the peak of sexual gratification. Your soft kisses sent me into a trance and the taste of your lips still linger on the tip of my tongue. Once you took charge, I remained motionless just gazing at your sexy eyes. I will always remember those moments whenever I will my eyes. You are the one I was looking for. ! Waiting for your reply Minnie.:)

Aleesha's reply came in back a few minutes.

Akash, you have left me speechless. Even after making love to you, I kept gazing at you and was left with no words. I love the way you lure me with your charm. I can still feel a tingling sensation between my legs. I felt as if I travelled to heaven today. As your hands touched me all over, the flames of passion, desire, and love took control over us. You slid your palm between my legs and I curled up with ecstasy. I pulled your hands away as I didn't want to finish it too soon. I wanted to experience pleasure slowly. When you came inside me, I knew you were the man I want to be with for the rest of my life. You complete me. Just thinking about how we made love makes me shiver. Keep caring for me always and never let your love fade away. I can't imagine living without you now. I trust you more than I trust myself. Love you always and hamesha. I hope you won't need scissors the next time around. You are such a cartoon, Mickey. Muahahhh! Gn.☺

Go Goa

Dabolim Airport, Goa, January 3, 2012

It was a sunny yet pleasant morning in Goa. Deep and Tamanna had landed at their destination along with Mr Verma and Kajal. Tamanna secretly hoped that being in a relaxing and romantic place like Goa would help bring Deep closer to her. Who knows, he may even develop feelings for her, bringing a new spark in her otherwise dull life. Their conference was scheduled at 11 am and they still had some time to relax in the beach town. They were going to stay at the Whispering Palms Beach Resort near Candolim Beach.

'What are your plans after the conference?' Kajal asked Tamanna who was sitting beside her in the cab on their way to the hotel.

'Not decided yet… I think we will…'

Tamanna was about to say something but was cut short by Deep.

'I think we should unwind and rest,' Deep said and looked at both the girls sitting in the back seat. Mr Verma was busy talking to someone on his phone.

Though Tamanna harboured feelings towards Deep, no one else in office had a hint about it. Tamanna wanted to make this trip memorable by expressing her feelings towards Deep once and for all. Deep on the other hand had finally decided not to think too much about Tamanna and her behaviour, even though the thought had haunted his mind from the day this trip had been announced. He had taken his decision and had something extremely serious to share with Tamanna which would put a full stop to all her thoughts and could even break all her dreams.

Both Mr Verma and Kajal were having a secret sexual affair, each for their personal benefit. Kajal gave him sexual pleasure and in the process satisfied her own financial and official needs. She had planned to cross all limits in the next couple of days and expected a heavy increment after this trip. Mr Verma, on the other hand, was a married man who knew how to take full advantage of the situation, and didn't mind giving her official benefits in return for fulfilling his desires.

How strange was the journey and how contradictory were their thoughts and relationships! As the car accelerated, all of them looked outside at the beautiful structures of Vasco. Goa was the place where everyone hoped to achieve what they desired in the next couple of days, but no one knew what could come their way. The next couple of days could answer many questions and leave their minds either clueless or take them to new heights of achievements, success, passion, and love.

The cab halted outside the hotel premises and everyone looked at each other, exchanging familiar plastic smiles.

They then moved towards their rooms with their luggage.

Tamanna relaxed as soon as she entered her Mediterranean-style room. She tied her hair into a knot and went outside to stand in the room's balcony. She was amazed to see the poolside view and imagined herself with Deep in the pool. She had decided to express her feelings to Deep that very night. The mere thought of it excited her since she was getting to spend quality time with Deep, away from the mad rush of the city.

'Are you going in for a bath?' Kajal asked Tamanna who was busy unpacking. Both of them were sharing the same room.

'You carry on. I will have my breakfast first. I am starving,' Tamanna replied. She picked up the menu card kept on the side table, ordered breakfast, and lied down on the bed, deeply immersed in thoughts.

She had never imagined that she would ever have such intense feelings for Deep whom she had trained some time back. She believed that Deep was financially unstable which was primarily restricting him from taking the first step towards her. Every man needs a woman when his life is in a mess. After all, life is just like a game of chess. The queen always protects the king. Tamanna had already appointed herself as the queen in Deep's life.

After their meeting in the conference hall of the hotel got over, they all had lunch together. Then they went back to their rooms to change into casuals since the plan was to explore the beaches of Goa.

Both the girls changed into short skirts and casual tops. Kajal was exposing for Mr Verma while Tamanna wanted to gain Deep's attention, as it was probably the first time Deep was going to see her exposed skin.

Deep had worn a white body fit T-shirt with Bermuda shorts which forced Tamanna to stare harder at his toned, muscular body. Mr Verma on the other hand had worn full-length track pants and a casual T-shirt in an attempt to look thinner.

'You look so sexy,' said Mr Verma holding Kajal by her waist as they walked outside the hotel premises.

Looking at them stroll like two lovebirds made Tamanna feel a bit jealous but nonetheless she was excited because she knew she just had to wait for a few more hours. They got into the cab and headed towards Baga beach.

'Tamanna, I have told the receptionist to book our tickets for the overnight casino cruise. So do not schedule anything after evening,' Mr Verma told Tamanna who was busy drinking a Bacardi breezer.

She had something different planned for the night. But she agreed to tag along as she felt proposing on a cruise accompanied by Goan music in the backdrop would be more romantic. Deep seemed disturbed by their idea of going on the cruise but he didn't utter a word. As they reached Baga beach, everyone ran towards the shore.

Deep relaxed on the shore with a beer bottle. Soon Tamanna too joined him. She was keeping an eye on Kajal and Mr Verma, observing their actions closely. She wanted to be in Deep's arms but he hardly cast a glance at her.

She was sitting right next to him, trying her best to get close to him, but he kept looking straight at the horizon. She even deliberately moved her skirt up exposing her thigh to seduce Deep but all in vain. It irritated Tamanna but she didn't want to break down in front of him. More than him, it was Kajal and Mr Verma's public display of affection that irritated her. Kajal was trying her best to seduce him and Mr Verma was lusting after her. Tamanna almost turned her face with disgust when she saw Mr Verma smooching Kajal in public! Their PDA was getting out of control!

She was upset by the fact that Deep had completely ignored her despite her sexy outfit. Each moment seemed like ages to her. As they travelled back to their rooms, Tamanna caught him looking at her which brought a smile on her face. Whatever be the reason, she loved it when he looked at her. He faked a smile wondering how he could avoid the cruise that night.

'What do you observe first in girls?' Mr Verma questioned Deep holding a glass of beer while having dinner at Tito's.

Tito's Courtyard was an informal, open-air dining restaurant.

'Now that depends on whether a girl is walking towards you or away from you,' Deep replied, half-drunk. They laughed at his statement and raised a toast.

'What you feel about Kajal?' Mr Verma asked him, putting his hand around Kajal's shoulder and getting closer.

'Sorry sir, I don't believe in shortcuts and relationships which are only for mutual benefit. I prefer to stay away from them,' Deep said looking at Kajal.

'Oh come on. Grow up. You should live life king size,' Mr Verma yelled.

Kajal stared at Deep as she knew Mr Verma had dismissed their relationship as mere enjoyment and nothing else. It was like a slap on her face. He hardly cared for her and continued to eat his food. All this while, Tamanna kept looking secretly at Deep and his last statement made her nervous.

After dinner, they decided to spend some more time on the beach before boarding the cruise.

'I am feeling unwell. I will rest in my hotel room for a while so that I can join you all on the cruise later. Otherwise I will feel uneasy on the cruise and will miss all the fun,' Deep exclaimed when they cleared the bill and came out of Tito's.

'Are you sure? I don't want you to miss the cruise Deep,' Tamanna said visibly concerned. After all she had planned a special night on the cruise for him.

He nodded but Tamanna insisted he stay back with them and not to go back to the hotel. Her continuous pampering was getting on his nerves.

'Don't worry Tammy. I will reach on time. Trust me. We will spend some good time together,' Deep told her in a sweet tone and gave her a seductive smile. Tammy told him to come on time.

Deep pretended that he was feeling uneasy due to the drinks he had consumed and left for the day. He ordered couple more bottles of beer in the room after taking a bath. He checked his mobile and saw 11 missed calls from Tammy. He wasn't shocked as it was quite typical of her. He ignored them and switched off his cell phone so that he could drink chilled beer sitting in the balcony of his room and enjoy Goa's weather.

After some drinks, he closed his eyes thinking about what would be the aftereffects of his decision to cancel the cruise plan. Even he wanted to talk about his life with Tamanna in all seriousness, but he felt that the cruise was not the right pace to do so. Goa was the right opportunity to tell Tamanna how he really felt but he never got a chance to be alone with Tammy anywhere. Thinking about the various probabilities, he dozed off on the chair in the balcony itself.

Meanwhile, the others were waiting for Deep to return so that they could board the cruise together.

Tamanna tried calling Deep a number of times but his phone was switched off. She was worried about him and cursed herself for allowing him to go back to the room.

'His cell is switched off. Should we go back to the room and check?' Tamanna asked Mr Verma.

'Leave it. He may not be feeling well. If we check on him now, we will miss our cruise,' Mr Verma said advising the girls to board the cruise.

Tamanna started walking towards the cruise with a heavy heart. She turned to look back every few seconds, hoping she would spot Deep running towards her. However, with each step she took, her dream seemed to evaporate in thin air. Deep was nowhere to be seen. Tamanna wanted to cry aloud as all her plans had shattered in a fraction of a second.

'Don't worry Tammy. I will reach on time. Trust me. We will spend some good quality time together.' His mesmerizing voice still reverberated in her head. A tear tolled down her eye and she couldn't believe it was for real. She was all alone in the midst of a crowd that seemed to be enjoying each other's company.

Kajal and Mr Verma were making the most of their time on the cruise. She looked gorgeous in her black one-piece dress and Mr Verma looked totally smitten by her as they danced to Goan music. Kajal had managed to fulfil her motive behind the Goa trip and even Mr Verma had not been left disappointed. However, for Tamanna the love game had now suddenly changed into an obsession. She had to achieve her love at any cost now. The intensity of Kajal and Mr Verma's love made her obsess more deeply about Deep. The night passed thinking about him but Tamanna decided to keep mum and not to react to Deep's betrayal.

The next morning when they left for the airport, Deep tried to talk to Tammy several times, but she kept ignoring him as his behaviour had made her even more upset. She tried to make him feel guilty for the previous night by avoiding him completely. Deep tried to convince her and explain the reason for his absence, but his half-hearted attempts failed to impress Tamanna. On the other hand, Kajal and Mr Verma had a satisfied look on their faces while returning back to Mumbai.

The Goa trip had ended on an ugly note for Deep and Tamanna and created rifts between them. Deep failed to share with her what was going on in his head. However it was getting difficult for Tamanna to ignore the feelings she had for Deep. The question was: How far would this obsession of hers take her?

Kisses and Misses

January 6

It was winter time. Aleesha decided to go out for a walk since Kritika was not in and room and she was feeling bored. She tried to call both Akash and Kritika but since neither of them picked up the phone, she went ahead by hereself. She walked towards the CCD outlet near her residence and decided to stop for a short coffee break. As she walked towards the outlet, she stopped short in her tracks. She turned around to see if someone was following her but there was no one to be seen. She ignored the weird vibe but somehow felt that something was not quite right. She started walking again. Once she entered CCD, she placed her order and took a seat at one of the vacant tables. One seated, she suddenly heard a familiar voice.

'You are amazing. I love the way you do things for me at odd hours, especially during the night,' said the voice.

With baby steps, she moved towards the cubicle in the corner of the café, meant for couples only.

'I love you so much for this. Thank you for accepting my proposal. You are the best,' said the same voice. This time Aleesha shivered.

As she went closer, she couldn't believe what she saw. If her heart was weak, she would have got a heart attack right there itself. Akash and Kritika were sitting at the table holding each other's hands.

Her body froze in shock and her mind tried to comprehend it all as the time ticked off on the clock. Her body began to tremble. Not once did she expect this to happen. Never in her wildest dreams would she have thought about being a witness to this. With a heavy heart and even heavier steps, she went closer to Akash who was equally shocked to see her. He didn't know how to react. He panicked and left Kritika's hands in a hurry, stammering to explain.

'How dare you? I mean how could you cheat on me and sit here with my friend? Akash I trusted you so much,' Alisha yelled.

She walked out of the cafe. In a flash, Akash ran behind her trying to make her understand the situation. But she did not have time for him and ran away sobbing.

Akash couldn't believe his luck. He stood there without moving an inch. All of a sudden all his plans and all the surprises had been shattered. Kritika came out running and inquired about Aleesha.

'Please explain to her that we didn't do anything wrong. I beg of you,' Akash pleaded with Kritika almost in tears.

Kritika just nodded and left. As she reached their room, she saw Aleesha sobbing on the bed. She was reading the message that Akash had sent to her after they made love for the first time. She saw Kritika coming in but pretended to ignore her. Kritika came near her bed and sat beside her.

Aleesha moved away from her saying she didn't want any clarification.

'Aleesha, please listen to me once. Whatever you saw was not the real picture. You know how much he loves you,' Kritika explained.

'I don't want any clarification. I shouldn't have trusted him. All boys are the same. They just want their desires fulfilled and nothing else. He has done it with me and moved on to the next girl. Tomorrow it will be someone else,' she said. She hardly listened to Kritika and kept yelling at her without bothering to even listen to any explanations.

She felt cheated. That's probably the most terrible thing. She thought of calling him but then decided to leave a message. She typed out a long message and was about to send it when she felt it was of no use. She deleted the message and threw the cell on the bed.

Lost in darkness, she kept thinking to herself—*Did he actually love me? I thought he had the same feelings and would protect me in the storm of life. It must be his charm that melted my heart or was it his gentle smile? But whatever it might be, one thing I know is that he does not feel the same for me anymore*. Tears kept rolling down her face. The reality of it broke her into pieces and it wounded her badly when she realized that Akash wanted to be with someone else. She couldn't believe that he could just move on without thinking about her feelings when he knew that she had done everything for him—supported him, comforted him, and loved him more than he loved himself. Then why did he choose to be unfaithful to her and hurt her like this?

It was around 11 pm. Kritika simply sat beside her silently. She didn't take much effort in explaining things to Aleesha. She had kept her fingers crossed as there were already too many misunderstandings and one mistake could brak Aleesha's trust completely.

Akash on the other hand didn't even bother calling up Aleesha up after his initial efforts to convince her failed. This frustrated Aleesha even more. Akash believed that the surprise he had planned for her would make her fall in love with him all over again. He waited for Kritika's instructions and was inquiring about Aleesha every few minutes.

Aleesha covered herself with a blanket but her tears didn't allow her to sleep. Kritika checked the time again. It was 11.45 pm and all the lights were switched off. Kritika called up Akash and gave him the go-ahead to enter their room. Aleesha could hear her whispering on the phone and she pulled the pillow over her head and covered her ears tightly with it.

Akash was inside the room the very next second. I followed him and latched the door. Aleesha saw us from under the blanket and couldn't control her temper. She picked up her bedsheet and threw it on Akash. It just fell short of landing on Akash's head. She started shouting on the top of her voice. We thought we would be caught, as someone would knock the door hearing Aleesha screaming so loudly. Kritika held her mouth shut and Akash took out red roses from his backpack. There were twelve roses in all tied into a bunch with a satin ribbon. He moved forward and offered the flowers to her. She was still angry at him and that was evident from the way she turned her face away wiping away tears from her face.

'What do you want now? You must have brought these for her, but seeing me, you are offering them to me?' Aleesha screamed.

I moved closer to Aleesha, held her by her arm, and made her sit down explaining everything to her. Akash was still standing while I convinced her and made her understand every minute detail of the incident. Akash had said I love you to Kritika for all the help she was offering for making the day special for Aleesha and him. They had no bad intentions whatsoever. They held each other's hand only for a fraction of a second, and that too because Akash was grateful for Kritika's help. It was only bad timing that Aleesha bumped into them at the same minute.

'Are you serious?' she asked me.

'Yes dear. Why should I lie to you? Trust me. It was just because he had planned something special for you today as you both complete six months of your relationship. At least smile now. It's not their fault. You simply misconstrued what had happened,' I said patting her back to make her smile.

Akash felt relieved when he saw Aleesha smile. He went down on his knees and presented the rose bouquet to her.

'I love you Minnie,' Akash said with a big smile.

Aleesha wiped away her tears and tried to smile when she said, 'I love you too.'

Akash got up and hugged her tightly after which Aleesha melted in his arms. She started crying like a kid and apologized for doubting his intentions and not trusting him. Akash kissed her earlobes and gave her a warm kiss on her forehead. Aleesha pulled her ears to apologize.

'You look cute when you cry and smile at the same time. I love you. Can you guess why I gave you twelve roses?' Akash questioned.

'Why Mickey?'

'Twelve roses are for our six months of togetherness. We completed six months happily and thus six roses…' Akash was about to continue but Aleesha interrupted.

'Then why twelve?'

'My jaan, six roses for making the last six months beautiful and six in advance because I believe we will complete a year in love too. Thus twelve roses complete the both of us,' Akash smiled.

They both hugged. The next moment their lips met, and their tongues explored each other's mouth. They were so lost in their kiss that they forgot that Kritika and I were standing right next to them. In the meanwhile, Kritika and I brought out the cake Akash had got along with him and kept it on the table.

'Guys, here is it. It's your time, let's celebrate it today,' Kritika said while I lit the candles.

'Wow. It's lovely. Akash, you are such a darling. You brought a Minnie and Mickey Mouse cake. So cute! Let me click a picture, ' Aleesha said taking a picture with her mobile phone and immediately uploaded it on her BBM.

'Make a wish and then blow off the candles in one go,' I instructed.

They looked at each other and then closed their eyes in order to make a wish. I believe that a silent wish should be made before blowing out the candles. If all the candles are put off in one breath, the wish will come true. They made a secret wish and then excitedly blew out all the candles in one go. While they were feeding each other small bits of the cake, it seemed the smoke from the candles carried their wishes and prayers to the almighty.

Real entertainment came in after cutting the two-tier cake. Aleesha decided to shove her piece of cake onto Akash's face.

'Ah!'

Kritika and I turned around to see Akash's face covered in chocolate and whipped cream. I waited to see Akash's reaction. He stood there with cake dripping down his T-shirt and Aleesha laughing uncontrollably. She took another piece of cake and swung it at Akash but he ducked and it hit Kritika instead.

'Oh gosh! I am so sorry,' Aleesha said.

Kritika immediately picked up a huge chunk and threw it on Aleesha but she ducked too and it came straight on my face. I grabbed the biggest piece I could get hold of and shoved it on Aleesha. She couldn't move and it her on her shoulders and face.

Aleesha stood atop a table and clearing her throat shouted, 'Cake Fight!'

At that moment, everyone started throwing cake pieces on each other. I went towards the stereo player and inserted a music CD to make the mood even more lively when I saw a piece zooming towards me. I ducked and it hit the wall this time. Everywhere Aleesha turned, she was hit with the cake. Her long hair was covered with white and pink cream, and chocolate.

'Stop throwing at me now,' she requested but Akash hit her on the chest and the cream went down her top.

'Aah! I AM SERIOUS,' she shouted wiping the cake sliding down under her top.

Kritika was approaching the cake fight differently. Every time the cake came her way, she caught it with her hand and ate it.

'This is crazy! We were supposed to be celebrating our six months anniversary and not wasting such a yummy ice-cream cake. I am putting an end to this,' Aleesha shouted peeping from under the bed.

'Stop this madness right now,' she continued but she was attacked with cake again. 'Ahhh!' She hid under the bed again, wiping the cake off her top.

Eventually the music stopped and everything came to a halt. However, I wondered how the girls would clean up the mess. It was going to be a tough task for them.

Akash went closer to Aleesha and hugged her as we were about to leave. He licked the cream off her face with his tongue and ate it.

'You know what tastes better than the cake on your face?' Akash questioned.

'What?'

'Your lips.' He pulled her towards him and kissed her passionately.

After cleaning up, we slowly moved out of the room under Kritika's guidance. As we sat in the car, Akash messaged Aleesha about another surprise.

Minnie, I hope you enjoyed my little surprise. I just wanted to shock you and make you feel special. I do care for you and will be there for you always. Never ever think that I will cheat on you or go out with someone else. You get hyper easily and overreact. Please stop assuming things and don't jump to conclusions without knowing the actual facts. It could harm our relationship in the future. Don't react to things so easily my jaan. I love you a lot and I am all yours. There is one more surprise waiting for you. I have kept a bag under your bed which has a gift for you. Tomorrow neither of us are going to office and college. I have taken a leave. We are going to spend time together recollecting the memories of our last six months. Once you see the gift I have kept in the bag, do message me. I am waiting.

Aleesha took out the bag kept hidden under her bed and removed a note and a gift-wrapped box from it.

The note said: Do wear it tomorrow. You will look no less than a princess in this.

She opened the bag to see a rich white chikan work Anarkali salwar kameez. The maroon churidar looked lovely while the white dupatta was in net with a ravishing red velvet border. She was on cloud nine and couldn't resist trying it. She immediately changed into her new outfit and looked in the mirror and blushed. She told Kritika to click some snaps of her on her BlackBerry and send it to Akash immediately. Aleesha was extremely happy and retired to bed with a smile on her face. Just before dozing off, she messaged him:

`Can't wait for tomorrow. I love you. Thank you for the amazing gift. I love it. I will come wearing it tomorrow just for you. I am really lucky to have someone like you in my life. Good night. Drive safe and give me a missed call when you reach home. Don't forget it, else I will kill you. I get worried when you don't. Love you.`

Akash and Aleesha were not a couple in love, they loved each other and thus they were a couple. Together they had submerged themselves in the ocean of love. For a woman, the proof of love is that she is willing to be destroyed by the one whom she loves. And Aleesha was no different. Though she sometimes lost her temper and would take rash decisions which hurt her emotionally, she still loved Akash. It was not a love story to be remembered for ages like Romeo and Juliet's, but was full of insecurities and possessiveness, and yet it was special in its own way.

January 7

Aleesha took the late pass from the warden since she was going to spend the evening with Akash. She called up Tamanna to inform her that she was going out with friends since she had told the warden that she was going to stay with her local guardian Tamanna.

'So where are you going?' Tamanna enquired on the phone.

'It's just a late evening party. My friends say its a surprise so I have no idea about the venue,' Aleesha replied.

'Oh! College friends?'

'Yes, also my boyfriend. Remember the guy I had told you about when we were in the disc? The one who was hitting on me? The same guy. We are dating now,' Aleesha blushed.

'Hmm,' Tamanna replied casually, like her love life did not matter to her. She hung up the phone to attend to some urgent matter.

Aleesha wore the dress Akash had gifted her. She looked fabulous in the white and red Anarkali. She had worn red stilettos with silver work on it and Kashmiri silver jhumke with small red stones at the centre that added to her beauty.

Akash and Aleesha had decided to meet at Mahalaxmi station. Aleesha boarded a local from Churchgate station. Her attire caught everyone's attention and all the other passengers kept looking at her. She reached the venue within 15 minutes and Akash was waiting for her outside the station on the bridge.

When Akash saw her coming towards him, he was floored by her beauty. She looked more beautiful than what he had imagined. She came near him and gave him a warm hug. He gazed at her carefully from head to toe.

'You ooze sex appeal in whatever you wear. You look so pretty, my love. You should wear Indian outfits,' Akash said still looking at her in wonder.

'It's you and your love which makes me feel beautiful. I have never felt this special before. And only you can handle me in my worst behaviour. Love you so much.' She knew her looks worked in her favour and had the power to floor Akash anytime she wanted. She knew she could be sensuous yet elegant at the same time.

Akash was dressed in black and dark red shaded silk Pathani. It looked trendy and at the same time made him feel masculine. He had worn the outfit with traditional pathani jootis.

'You look no less than a Nawaab today. Just look at you! Killer! Your cute dimples make you so tempting that I so want to eat you right now. I hate the fact that you can seduce me so easily,' she teased him as they moved towards Haji Ali.

The crowd of pedestrians blocked their path. The worship place is thronged by numerous pilgrims and worshippers every day. Irrespective of faith and religion, people pay their homage to get the blessings of the legendary saint. They tried to make their way between hawkers and pedestrians. There were vendors selling earrings, necklaces, and bangles. Shouts of '*paanch ka do*' were more prominent than the crashing waves. The 500-metre long walkway seemed like a gateway to heaven with water surrounded it on all the sides. The sea waves crashed on the rocks near the pathway at lightning speed. The taste of the seawater lingered in their mouths as they climbed the steps to the Dargah.

'Akash, I can feel such positive vibes here. I am in love with this place,' Aleesha whispered.

They entered the Dargah which had a tomb covered by a brocad red and green sheet supported by a delicate silver frame. Aleesha glanced in all the directions and was enthralled looking at the tomb. She felt heavenly. The wind carried the mesmerizing fragrance of attar. The marble pillars inside the main hall were decorated with multihued mirrors and it embraced the ninety-nine names of Allah. There was a big chandelier right above Haji Ali's tomb.

'Cover your head with a dupatta and let's wish for something for us,' Akash suggested looking straight into Aleesha's eyes.

She nodded in agreement. Akash removed a white scarf from his pocket and tied it on his head. He bowed down in respect, touching the tomb with his hands, and kissing it in devotion. He tied a thread around one pillar and asked a mannat. The sweet smelling smoke from the lobaan and incense sticks had made the atmosphere thick and cloudy. The person sitting beside the tomb gently patted their heads and shoulders with a bunch of peacock feathers and they felt as if all their pain had subsided in that one moment.

Akash closed his eyes and prayed:

'You have shown me both sides of life. When I hardly knew what the world is, you took away my father and left me with no one to share my feelings. And then I met Aditya. I thank you whole heartedly for giving me such a friend who has always been with me even during my bad times. Then, you brought Aleesha into my life and I felt complete. I could share everything with her which I used to keep hidden from myself. For her, I have three wishes. I hope this time too you will fulfil them. Firstly, you know very well that we fight over small things but we love each other as much. Therefore, God, please make us forget our previous day's fights when we wake up the next morning. Secondly, God please instill a bit more discipline in me so that I don't throw a wet towel on the bed after a shower, or I keep shoes in the shoe rack, and clean all the mess I make while cooking. I don't want Aleesha to get irritated by my habits. And thirdly, please fulfil all that Aleesha wishes for and make her happy so that she chooses me above any other guy.'

When he opened his eyes, it gave him a feeling of salvation. He looked at Aleesha who still had her eyes closed. He gazed at her while she prayed for him:

'I know that I am a bit immature God, but my love for Akash is real. I know we still have a long way to go, but I want to be with Akash forever. Bless Akash and me so that we may never surrender to whatever challenges that come our way. Fill our hearts with love for each other and make us realize each other's worth. I have heard that you don't upset anyone who prays here and turn everyone's wish into a reality. It may sound a bit kiddish, but God I have three wishes. Firstly, do some magic so that no other girl likes Akash; you know he is a bit popular among girls. Even Akash should not like any other girl except me for his entire life. Secondly, even if we both lose our teeth and our hair turns grey, we should still love each other the same way we do now. And thirdly, I know I am mad that I jump to conclusions without giving it so much as a thought and fight with Mickey a lot. But please, please, please never let us sleep without hugging one another after a fight. I hope you will listen to my prayers and help me turn them into reality.'

Aleesha opened her eyes slowly with a smile on her face and turned her face towards Akash who was gazing at her.

She told him to close his eyes, look straight ahead, and pray for a happy life together.

After praying for each other and taking the blessings of Haji Ali, they came outside to eat something at the Haji Ali Juice Centre. Akash took the menu card in his hand and placed an order for two paneer rolls and mango cream. The seating was limited but they were lucky enough to get a table. Aleesha sat on a chair and searched her bag for something.

'What are you looking for?' Akash enquired gulping down one spoon of the cream.

'If you can surprise me, can't I? I have been saving money for this. Not even Kritika knows about it. I wanted to keep it a secret but never thought you would remember,' Aleesha said holding his hands and kissing them.

'Should I open it now?' Akash asked trying to feel what was inside the gift packet. It was a bit heavy and he couldn't guess what it was.

'Not now. Open it only once you reach home, please? Anyhow, it's not something you can open here,' Aleesha said with a smile.

After having their rolls and mango cream, they moved towards Mahalaxmi station. They had decided to spend the evening in the Cyprus area of Mulund. They were sitting in the garden recollecting all the memories of their togetherness. They laughed at all the funny moments they had shared with each other. As they rejoiced, they came and sat closer to each other on the bench. The place was not very crowded, allowing them to feel the heat of their love. Aleesha pressed her body against his, and gave him a love bite on his neck.

'Ouch!' he muttered in pleasure. Akash pressed his lips on hers, sucking them slowly and passionately. His hands were probing under her Anarkali suit.

In between their sensual romance, Aleesha managed to free her lips from his and whispered slowly in his ear, 'Jaan, you are the reason for butterflies inside my stomach. I get them every time I am with you. You are the reason for my smile and the glow on my face. I don't need any beauty parlours to get this glow. Your kisses can make my face glow even in the saddest moments. Never break my trust, Akash. Just be the same always.'

Akash didn't reply but just gave her a big dimpled smile. They remained in the same position for almost half an hour and then decided to leave.

Akash unwrapped the gift once he reached home. It was a bed sheet with matching cushion covers with their pictures on it. He had never expected such a warm gift from her. He immediately changed the cushion covers and the bed sheet and clicked a picture to send to her. The bed cover had a message written on it—*My Mickey, my cutie, and my hottie... you mean the world to me. Your smile brings brightness in my life. You are mine and only mine. I love you jaan.*

Seedhe saadhe saara sauda seedha seedha hona jee
Maine tumko paana hai ya tune main ko khona jee
Aaja dil ki kare saude baazi kya narazi..
Aa re aa re aa re aa!

He latched the door of his room and felt the warmness of the bed sheet and the cushions. He loved the gift to the core and messaged Aleesha to thank her:

`One of the photos on the pillow makes me remember the day we took a bubble bath together. I am so much in love with that pic. The look on your face is simply amazing. I can spend all my life looking at it. I am so lucky to have you in my life. I never expected something so beautiful that would bring all the memories of our past in front of me in one flash. Our first meet, our first kiss, the day when we made love, our bubble bath, funny moments of our good times together and what not. Wow! Am going crazy smiling looking at all the photos. Muaaaaa!! I wish you could sleep with me on this bed right now and make love to me. Oh God!! Just the thought of it is sending shivers down my spine. I will never break your trust. You are my cutie pie, my Minnie. Love you so much!!!`

It was a dream that they held on to with all their heart. All his life Akash had dreamt of someone who would make him smile and take him into a fantasy world. The dream had turned into a reality when he saw Aleesha on the first day. Now this fantasy was waiting for its happy ending.

Life was not easy with all its burdens, but when Akash and Aleesha were together, no drama was hard to handle and no burden was hard to bear. Life wasn't a fairytale romance, but they had the support of each other, and that is all they wanted.

From Ashes to Ashes

January 13

It was almost a fortnight since they had returned from Goa but still Tamanna kept ignoring Deep. Their conversations were restricted only to office work. Her silence made Deep more anxious and left him baffled. He knew there was something cooking in her mind but he couldn't figure out what.

Tamanna was sitting at her desk with her pen stuck in her mouth, thinking about Deep. Though she wanted to show she couldn't have cared less, the truth was she cared for him deeply. Although she had lost out one opportunity, she was waiting for another right time to tell him. She started typing on her phone:

Every morning, I think I need you, your fragrance, and your smile around me. If you look at me only once, I'd be your slave for life. I don't just want to hold your hand—a part of me wants to set you on fire and hold you closer while the flame consumes us both. I want to kiss your heart so I know that only I possess it entirely. I sense your presence

```
even while laughing and talking with others as
if an invisible chord runs straight from my
heart to yours. You are tied down deep inside
my head and I play my crazy love games on you
without even letting you know. If I let you
know everything I feel, can you handle my love
and madness? Will you satisfy my thirst the
same way you do inside my mind when I satisfy
myself?
```

She went near Deep's desk and ordered him to stay back in office after work hours for a client meeting. Deep nodded in agreement as he took it as an opportunity to reveal what was going on in his mind. He couldn't take it anymore.

Finally, the time is here. Today, I will tell her all about my life and will apologize for having hurt her. I know I might lose my job because of this, but I don't have any other choice, he thought.

The clock ticked away slowly. Tamanna counted each minute and mentally went over all that she had planned for the evening. She went to Mr Verma who was busy in scheduling meetings and asked for a few minutes of his time.

'Mr Verma, I am supposed to go to for a client meeting and office cabs are not available. So can you…'

'You need not worry. You can take my car. Provided you have a license,' Mr Verma joked while handing his car keys to Tamanna.

He obliged expecting Tamanna would return the favour with interest sometime in the future. After all, Tamanna was a beautiful girl with a great body which was good enough to tempt Mr Verma.

'Mr Verma, should we drop you home? We are going via Andheri.'

'I think you carry on. I will be late. Just take care of the car. By the way, who you are going with?' he enquired.

When Tamanna told him that she was going with Deep, Mr Verma gave her a naughty smile. She didn't react but just nodded and left. Each step towards Deep was an indication of how desperately she wanted him in her life. It wouldn't be wrong to say that she was somewhat addicted to his manly voice and personality.

Tamanna briefed him about the meeting without telling him about the venue, saying that it was not only important on a professional level but also on a personal level, since it never hurts to know your co-employees a little better. She even told him that this meeting could open new doors for him. Deep couldn't understand what she was referring to. Only she knew that she actually meant it could open the door of romance in their lives. Tamanna's each step was forcing Deep to let the cat out of the bag.

Tamanna kept driving silently, navigating through the traffic of Navi Mumbai. Deep was getting anxious to know where they were heading. They had passed Nerul and she still hadn't halted yet. He tried his best to remain calm and not question her unnecessarily. However, once they passed Khargar, Deep grew impatient and inquired, 'Where exactly is the meet? It will be too late for you to travel back home so late I suppose.'

'It's okay, Deep. I don't mind it as long as I am with you,' Tamanna said and winked at him.

Before he could react, Tamanna's phone rang. He could clearly hear her telling someone that she had reached Andheri and had parked the car safely. Deep found it strange that she was lying to someone about the location. By now he was completely confused about what was happening. He sensed something was wrong. One thing he was very sure of was that there was no client meeting at all.

'So there is no meeting, right?' he asked anxiously.

'There is. A meeting is scheduled. The only difference is that it's not an official one. It's our personal meeting. Just you and me,' she said slowing down the car.

'So where are we going? Why did you lie to me?' Deep screamed. He was losing his temper but controlled himself because he thought that he couldn't get a better opportunity to talk to Tamanna about certain things that had been on his mind. He quickly changed his tone and said, 'Even if you had told the truth, I would have come. After all, you are not only my manager but a good friend too. Am I wrong, Tammy?'

She nodded and reached out for his hand. Deep felt a bit uncomfortable when she came close to him, but he knew he had to bear it a little longer for his own sake. If he would have shown even slight resistance, she could have lost control of the car. He knew very well that Tamanna hated rejection. He remained silent, all the while wishing they reach the destination soon. He was still clueless about where exactly they were heading to and Tammy's constant touches irritated him. She even massaged his thighs and rolled her fingers over his jeans which made him restless. He was about to scream in anger when they reached the destination.

He read the board next to a grocery shop which said 'Shiravli Village'. It was a place near Panvel.

Tammy got down from the car and went to the shop. Deep feared something unexpected might happen and he thought of informing his friend about it, but things were happening so quickly that he couldn't think straight. Tamanna returned with a plastic bag that she kept on the back seat. Deep tried to figure out what was in it but quickly couldn't. As Tamanna started driving again, Deep looked outside the window trying to find out where they were going. The car stopped in front of a big gate which had a nameplate beside it.

'Khanna cottage'. It looked like a farmhouse. Deep's heartbeats increased and he crossed his fingers trying to guess what would happen next. He somehow kept calm as he wanted to make his point clear today anyhow. A caretaker opened the door and Tamanna parked the car inside. They got down from the car and she told him to follow her.

The sun had set and it was getting dark. The bizzare silence of the small village of Shiravli frightened both Deep and Tamanna. It made them more anxious and impatient, though for different reasons. After being ditched in Goa, Tamanna's infatuation had increased even more. For Deep, it was like a nightmare from which he wanted to wake up at the earliest. They both went inside the farmhouse after parking the car in the lawn.

Once inside, Tammy took out bottles of whiskey and vodka from the plastic bag and placed them on the table.

'Tammy, please explain what's all this? It's getting on my nerves now,' Deep said asking for a clarification.

'I wanted to tell you something from a long time but never got the chance to do so. I am sorry that I had to lie to you, but I don't have any wrong intentions. Please relax and settle down. Just give me some time to change, as I am feeling uncomfortable in these formal clothes. I'll join you in 15 minutes,' said Tamanna and went to change in the room.

Deep tried to act as normally as possible since he not only wanted to save his job but his dignity as well. He removed his handkerchief and wiped the sweat from his forehead. He was extremely nervous and had anticipated what was coming his way. He kept thinking of various ways to defend himself and save his job.

His family flashed in front of him and he kept thinking about being jobless. It was not that his financial condition was weak, he kept thinking about what his dad had to go through when his company shut down suddenly and he went into depression when the income flow stopped. That depression had become the very cause of his death, as he could never find employment again. However, those days were different and there were many new opportunities nowadays. This was one of the reasons why Deep was very professional in his work and never liked taking shortcuts to achieve professional success. He was extremely sincere in his work and never ever thought that one day he would have to face such a situation in his life where he would have to fight with his phobia to be loyal to his personal commitments. He couldn't resist the temptation and served himself a drink, gulping it in one go. He had gathered courage to speak his heart out today and waited for Tamanna to join him.

He was making another glass for himself when Tamanna opened the door and came and stood next to the sofa. She had changed into a pair of slacks and a loose green top. She walked towards the table and poured herself a drink. Deep was stunned to look at her behaviour. He was not only shocked but also surprised at her posture while she sat in front of him sipping the drink. She had a spark in her eyes which he had never seen before. She kept the glass on the table and gazed at him. Deep tried to take his eyes off her but couldn't resist looking at her since she looked so alluring. Tamanna knew exactly what she had to do. She went closer to Deep and sat beside him. Deep moved away slightly but she covered the space by shifting slightly to his side.

'Are you okay? I don't think we should do this. We shouldn't cross our limits of friendship,' Deep muttered. She was inching closer to him and soon her lips almost met his. There was hardly any space between them.

'Deep, why do you always think about imposing limits? Do I ever stop you from doing anything? I have been wanting to tell you something for a long time now,' she said and relaxed on the sofa.

'There is some string attached between us that brings me closer to you every time you smile at me. As we slowly got to know each other, I started daydreaming, thinking about us taking long walks, holding hands, kissing each other, and doing everything that lovers do—from gentle kisses to passionate moans. I have waited so long to express what I feel, but failed every time due to some or the other reason. I had planned to tell you everything in Goa too but you fell ill and I had to drop my plan. I'll do whatever you want but accept me in your life. I never thought that I could love someone so much. Believe me when I say this, I can cross any limits to make you mine. But Deep, no matter what happens, I'll always love you until the end of time. Just touch me once and make me yours. Touch every part of my body and set it on fire. I need you. I need you for all the little things we do in life. Now that I've found you, will you be mine forever? Trust me Deep, I never knew love like this before,' she said.

She came closer to him, so close that she almost fell on him, and said, 'Please Deep, say something. I want to know what you feel about me. For God's sake, don't be quiet. I want to hear you say 'I love you Tammy'. Deep, I beg of you. Don't you love me? Don't you feel that I am beautiful? Look at me. Look at every inch of my body. Isn't it curvy and sexy enough to turn you on? If yes, then let me hear you say that. Every day I dream of you saying those words but today I want to hear it for real...' She went on and on until Deep sealed her lips. Not with his lips but with his fingers. She moaned slightly as his fingers touched her wet lips.

'Listen carefully. I need to tell you something extremely important which can shatter both our lives, but I have to,' Deep muttered and got up from the sofa and walked towards the window with the glass of drink in his hand. It scared Tammy to such an extent that she sat emotionless observing each of his movements.

'Tammy, it's not possible. I mean are you getting what I am saying?' He moved towards her and continued, 'I lost my dad at early age. I am the only son in my family and I can't mix my professional and personal life. I know you feel it's weird for me to think in such a way but yes, I can't go beyond our friendship and be your life partner. I don't want people talking about us in office or pointing out fingers at me, the way they do with Kajal. People are too narrow-minded when it comes to such relationships. They don't understand the depth of any relationship. They just need some hot topic to discuss and I don't want to be the topic of such discussion. Therefore, I think we should stop here. Moreover, I knew what you were upto. You had already expressed your feelings towards me in the taxi when you were drunk. I don't think you remember because you were not in your senses. Thus, I tried to keep some distance whenever you tried to open up your heart to me. But it's high time now and I don't want to raise your hopes. I never combine my personal and professional life. I have always maintained a gap between the two and never shared anything with you about my personal commitments. I don't know if you will believe me or not but I am already committed. It's been more than six months now and I can't betray her and break her trust by doing such things with you. I love her a lot, so much so that whenever I am not engrossed in official work, I am either with her or thinking about her. No one else can be on my mind apart from her. I am madly in love with her. I should have told you this long before when I came to know about your intentions, but I never got the chance. The couple of times I did get an opportunity, I chickened out for unknown reasons. I hope you understand my position. We are friends and will continue to be so. However, please don't act like this. It will force me to break friendship with you.' He sat on the sofa and gulped another glass of drink. He closed his eyes and relaxed for a bit as he had finally managed to clear things with Tammy without the fear of losing his job.

Tamanna couldn't believe what she had heard. She stood there completely numb as a wave of terror swept over her. All her dreams had shattered in a few minutes. She felt fear creeping over her.

'Deep you can't do this. Do you even know how much I love you,' she said moving closer to Deep. Alcohol had completely taken over her. She was becoming a bit aggressive now in trying to force him to change his mind.

'From day one, it has just been you. Do I look like a slut to you? I have never ever allowed anyone to touch me because I have always dreamt to be with you. I want you to touch me first and no one after that can even dare to do it again. You just can't walk away shattering all my dreams and wishes! I can't let you go. Not so easily. I know even you lust for my body and desire my love. You just don't want to accept the reality. You want to run away from it to your dream world where you sleep with that bitch. Move on Deep, come close to me…feel me…feel my body… Please don't break my heart today. I have waited for so long…not now,' she said and hugged him tightly.

'Tammy, stop it! Are you out of your mind? I've already told you I don't love you. I am committed,' Deep said raising his voice, but Tamanna barely moved an inch. She rested her head on his chest.

'Deep, don't stop yourself. I'll give you whatever you want. But don't leave me like this. I need you. I love you and I can't even imagine my life without you. Please Deep… I want…'

'Fuck off...you have lost it,' he shouted and pushed Tamanna so hard that she fell on the sofa. He continued, 'How many times should I tell you that I don't feel anything for you? I love my girlfriend too much. I think you won't understand like this. Let me show you our pictures.'

He went closer to Tamanna and took out his cell phone from his shirt pocket. He opened his mobile's gallery and showed her various pictures of of him with his girlfriend. The pictures left Tamanna speechless. They were of no one else but ALEESHA! She was the girl Deep was dating! She looked at the pictures carefully and then at Deep. Before she could speak, Deep screamed at her, 'You know her, right? Now do you believe what I said or should I bring her in front of you? We are completely in love with each other and no third person can come between us. Neither you nor my profession. I never let your hopes go up, but the way you are behaving is disgusting. There is a limit to everything and you have crossed all limits. Do whatever you want, but I am going. I can't stay here even for a minute.'

He took his bag and started walking towards the main door. Tamanna got up and tried to stop him but he was too strong for her. He didn't even look at her and left the place, leaving her heartbroken, disillusioned, and dejected. She had lost the battle of love. She couldn't control her temper and threw the glass in anger. She even broke some of the showpieces kept in the living room and screamed loudly, sobbing in pain.

She was in complete shock, and kept on gulping glasses of alcohol and inhaling drugs. She couldn't take this loss. Deep had turned her fears into reality and ripped her heart into pieces. Her smile vanished and deep melancholy took over her. She lost herself when she lost him. She realized that their paths were different and they could never meet again.

'You just played with my emotions and now it's all over. You left without even looking at me and without even thinking of my pain once. You swept me out of your life like dust on the floor. I gave you all that you wanted but you didn't even care once. You walked away and didn't even turn back. Should I think that you just used me? Or was I a fool to support you when you didn't even speak a word to me? If such is the case, then one day you will be sorry for what you have done to me. I'll not let you go away so easily. If you can't be mine, then I'll make sure you can't be with anyone else. I'll make you beg for my love. I'll make sure you lose everything you have and come back to me so that I can give you everything you want...'

She took out her cell phone from her purse. She looked at the screen and saw an unread message. She ignored it and called Deep but he didn't answer. After several calls, his phone became unreachable. This irritated her and she screamed out loudly.

'If you can't be mine then I'll make sure you can't be with anyone else either. I'll make you beg for my love. I'll make sure you lose everything you have and come back to me so that I can give you everything you want...'

She kept on repeating those words. She was unaware of what she was doing, and every second, the intake of drinks was killing her from within. She scrolled her contacts list and saw Aleesha's name on top. She thought for a moment and then called her. It was too late but she kept on calling her until she picked up.

'Hi Tammy di, how are you? Why are you calling me so late at night?' Aleesha asked.

'So I shouldn't call you at this hour? Or you are making out with your boyfriend?' Tamanna shouted.

'What? Are you drunk? How dare you…'

'Shut up! How dare you… You didn't even think once how I would feel? Not even once? I helped you so much when Mumbai was an alien city for you. You forgot everything and played dirty games on me?' she screamed.

'What are you saying Tammy di? I am…'

'Don't dare to open your mouth, you bitch. If I had known that you were a slut, I would have... And you think your boyfriend will keep you happy? You think he won't ever ditch you? Your boyfriend has left me alone… You might not know that he worked with me in my office. But today, he tried to force me to be physical with him. When I didn't agree, he tried to force himself upon me. Somehow, I managed to protect myself… these guys won't ever understand us and will continue to play with our emotions. I am warning you to stay away… the rest is up to you. You decide whether to trust me who supported you every time, or trust a guy who has just come in your life and is pretending to be loyal to you. He is a big time cheat who loves playing with the emotions of girls and misuses them as mere toys.'

Tamanna disconnected the call before Aleesha could say anything. Aleesha on the other hand was completely taken aback after all that Tamanna had said. She called Akash but his cell phone was unreachable and she dropped him a message. Aleesha tried calling Tamanna several times but she didn't answer because not only was her cell on silent mode, but the effect of drugs had taken a toll on her. Aleesha was left helpless, with no choice but to wait for the morning to know what was happening.

Tamanna walked outside and opened the door of the car. She sat in the driver's seat but could hardly open her eyes. She had put the car on first gear and pressed on the accelerator when she saw a light flashing on her cell phone. It was Aleesha again. She disconnected the call and saw an unread message symbol blinking on the screen. She thought of reading it while driving but her phone stopped working. She threw the phone on the side seat and raced the car through the darkness of Shiravli village with the thoughts of revenge running in her mind and tears rolling down her eyes. She was breathing heavily as she felt the pain in her heart.

She recollected the moments she had spent with Deep. Her head spun like a merry-go-round and she could not understand how Deep had given up on the opportunity to be with her. She cursed herself even more for not asking Aleesha about her personal life. She always remained aloof, lost in her own thoughts and beliefs. At least she could have once asked Deep if he was committed. At least she could have enquired from someone in office whether he was dating someone or not. At least she could have asked Aleesha when she called to say she was going out with her friends. All these thoughts kept running in her mind and tears kept rolling down her cheeks. Slowly her eyesight became weak and everything seemed blurred. She kept her foot the accelerator and raced on through the flyover at Khargar near 'Three Star' hotel. The streetlights were off, but still she continued to drive rashly, taking out all her frustration and anger on the accelerator. The car was running at a speed of more than 100 kmph even in the darkness. The darkness that Deep had filled in her life made her shiver. She was trying to fix all the pieces of her life to get a clear picture of all the incidents that had occurred in the past few months. The more she stressed her mind, the more she sobbed and her vision became more and more blurred.

Her cell phone had started working again, so she picked it up to read the unread message. There were no vehicles on the road and Tamanna was driving at a breakneck speed. It was Deep. Her heart pumped faster and her shivering turned intense. Even though she could hardly read what was written on the screen she tried doing that while the car was racing at the speed of 110 kmph. She looked down read and:

`Tammy please don't take me wrong...` She brought the screen closer to her eyes, and pressed her foot on the accelerator, which made the car gain maximum speed. She started reading again:

`Tammy please don't take me wrong. My intention was not to hurt...`

The car skidded towards the left and then towards the right. She had lost control of the car completely.

Screeeeeeeeeeeeeetchhhhhh!!! The car crashed onto the divider with a loud bang. The car bumped into the divider at full speed and rolled over twice on the road.

Disappointment, disbelief, and fear filled her mind as she lay on the side of the road struck inside the car. The weight of the car pressed down on the lower half of her body with monstrous force. She couldn't move. Everything had happened so quickly. She lay there trying her best to comprehend what had happened. She saw some cars driving by and tried to yell but found it difficult to scream. She could feel the bitter taste of blood in her mouth. She struggled to move but the car was thrashed so badly that she couldn't lift a finger. Every minute seemed like a lifetime. She was counting her last breaths and had closed her eyes gasping like a fish out of water. She waited for someone to help her out.

Everything had come to a standstill in the last few hours of Tamanna's life. The dark side of her was probably hidden due to her introvert nature.

It's rightly said that when you are in love, you should throw caution to the winds. Tamanna had taken the saying too seriously and it had landed her here, in the midst of a debris with no one to help her out.

It's not falling that hurts, it's that sudden halt at the end that does.

Love isn't addiction, it's the attachment and obsession that causes destruction.

The saddest truth in all this chaos was that Tamanna had closed her eyes forever, leaving behind many unanswered questions.

Price & Prize of Professionalism

Nervousness filled Deep's heart when he left for office early next morning. He didn't have the courage to face Tamanna and kept wondering if she has created any more havoc after he had left her at the farmhouse. Disturbed, he reached the office premises. While taking the lift, he kept thinking about all the negative probabilities that could have happened in the last few hours which could adversely affect his career. But never in his wildest dreams could he have imagined being greeted by police once he reached office. Unknown to Deep, they had come to investigate Tamanna's death. As he reached the work floor, he was made to sit in front of some police officers who bombarded him with a number of questions related to Tamanna.

'What's wrong?' Deep asked in a state of shock.

'Mr Deep, where were you last night?' the cop asked him.

'With Tamanna ma'am. We had gone for a client meeting. But why are you asking?' he asked anxiously.

'You need to come along with us to the police station for enquiry,' the officer said.

'But what's the matter?'

'Tamanna is dead. We found her body near the Nerul highway. We went through her stuff and came to know from her office id that she worked here. Though it was an accident, we have also come to know that the car she was driving belonged to a Mr Verma. He stated that she was with you since yesterday evening. So where were you when the accident took place? Mr Verma said that Tamanna had told him that she was going to Andheri for the meeting. Then how did she reach Navi Mumbai? Your other co-employee Kajal also said that there were some conflicts between you both, even in Goa during your official trip. So I'm going to straightway ask you since I think you can answer all these questions better. We want to investigate whether it was just an accident or was she forced to take such a step because of sexual harassment or rape. We have already sent the body for post-mortem, and the medical reports will soon clear the picture. Before that we need some clarification on all the accusations your colleagues are making on you.' Deep was standing there dumbstruck. He could hardly make eye contact with anyone in office because only he knew the truth. The rest of them simply chose to believe what Tamanna had told them. The cops took him along with them to the police headquarters. He was going to pay the price for his professionalism.

He felt embarrassed at the close scrutiny, like a caged animal in the zoo, stared at by everyone. Deep couldn't believe his fate and was stunned by the news of Tamanna's death. He could remember the way Tamanna had cursed him the previous night. He quietly went and sat in the police jeep as instructed. He wished he could reach the police station as soon as possible so that he would save himself from the constant stares. Never in his worst nightmare had he imagined that one day he would sit in a police jeep and be taken away as a prime suspect behind someone's death. He wished he could have handled the situation last night in a better fashion. Sitting in the jeep, he kept thinking how his one harsh decision had taken away someone's life. Every minute seemed like an hour in the jeep, making him feel like a criminal. He wondered what really killed Tamanna. The accident? The betrayal? Or him? Or was it Tamanna herself? All he wanted was to make Tamanna realize that he was committed to someone else. He wanted to do everything for his love, but never wanted Tamanna to meet with such an awful end.

The jeep halted outside the police station and the cops dragged him inside. As Deep sat on the chair, the officer shot his first question.

'Mr Deep, did you have an affair with her? How did she reach Nerul? Was it a planned murder after sexual molestation which was made to look like an accident?'

'Please officer, I didn't do anything. I am innocent. I didn't even know that Tamanna met with an accident. I came to know about it only once I reached office today. Please trust me officer. I'll tell you everything that happened,' Deep stammered.

'You better speak the truth and don't try to hide anything from us. And anyway, we will find the truth behind this accident sooner or later. So better speak the truth, save our time, and save yourself from getting behind the bars if you are innocent. Also, let me tell you before you start your story that we might get your narcoanalysis done, and if your statement differs, you'll be in big trouble,' the officer warned Deep and told one of his juniors to record his statement.

Deep was shivering badly. He picked up the glass of water kept on the table. He wiped his sweat before speaking. He narrated the entire incident which had taken place the day before.

'Trust me sir, I never loved her and never knew she had such strong feelings for me. I just felt that she was attracted to me and nothing else. Then that night she told me that she was madly in love with me. I didn't even touch her but she tried forcing herself on me, forcing me to leave the place even before the accident had taken place. I walked for a few miles and spotted a cab coming in my direction. I hailed for it to stop and asked the driver take me back home. Tamanna still kept calling me repeatedly which irritated me further and in this state of anger, I threw my mobile in the creek when the cab was crossing Mulund Bridge. Next morning, I realized that I didn't have my cell phone with me and with that I had lost all my contacts too. Thus, I was one of the last people to know about Tamanna's death. I am not hiding anything. I swear, sir. I am nowhere involved in it. Moreover, she was drunk really badly and I think that had something to do with her death. She had even taken drugs. Before you ask me, I want to tell you that even I drank in moderation, but I did not go overboard like her. You can take my tests if you want. Please sir, believe me.'

'Since when have you been working in Tamanna's team?' the officer asked.

'Since the day I joined the company, sir. She never interacted much with anyone but always hinted that she liked me. Every time something weird happened between us, I would tell my best friend about it. The only mistake I did was the I hid the fact that I was in a relationship and committed to someone else. But I never had any bad intentions towards her.'

All through his question-answer session, Deep failed to notice the girl sitting on a chair behind him. She was listening to their conversation carefully.

'So for how long have you been working in Galaxy House and why do you sign on your documents with an 'A' in the beginning? ' questioned the officer turning the pages of the file containing Deep's official documents. 'Are you Aleesha?' the policeman asked the woman sitting behind Deep. He asked the girl to come in front and sit next to Deep. Deep however didn't turn his head since he wanted to get out of the mess as quickly as possible.

'It's been around eight months now. And yes, the 'A' in my signature is my first name. My friends and close ones, including my family members, call me by that name. My dad, who is no more in this world, kept my name. However, for official purposes, I prefer to use my middle name, Deep.'

Aleesha was texting someone on her phone while she made her way to the table when she heard the officer say, 'So what's your first name? And did Tamanna know about it?'

'No sir. Tamanna did not know about it. I didn't feel the need to tell her as we were friends and nothing more,' he replied turning his head towards the girl who was about to take a seat. His heart stopped beating as he came face to face with Aleesha. The blood in his veins froze. How desperately he wanted to get out from there.

Aleesha saw him and seemed lost in thoughts.

How can this be possible? Why did he do this to me? Was Tamanna speaking the truth last night? Was that the reason why she called me up to tell me everything? How can he sexually assault Tammy di and why? Was I not good in bed? Did he ever love me?

'Mr Deep, I asked you something,' the officer reminded him.

'Yes sir, 'A' stands for Akash,' he stammered.

'So I'm guessing your full name is Akashdeep—AKASH and DEEP?'

'Yes sir,' he somehow managed to say, stealing a glance at Aleesha, but her face was expressionless.

The feeling of being in love is so intense that it feels like it will last forever. Aleesha couldn't believe that he didn't feel the same way as she did. She couldn't believe that this sacred relationship has been destroyed. She was sure that they understood and loved each other a lot. Now the feelings of betrayal and hurt had left her soul empty and deceieved.

'Aleesha, do you know this guy?' the officer asked.

She thought to herself, *I think I should tell the truth to the cops. Should I tell them that Tammy di had called me up last night and had confessed that he had forced himself upon her? But I love him. How can I? No, I can't. Or should I? Oh God, why me? Though he has made a fool out of me, I can't do that to him. I can't disrespect my love. I wish I did not love him so that I could punish him for all the pain he caused to Tammy Di. If I do the same thing as him, what's the difference between my love and his betrayal? That's it. I can't.*

'No! I don't know him,' she said staring at him with tears rolling down her cheeks.

'Ms Aleesha, tell me something—did this guy ever visit Tammy when you stayed with her or did she ever discuss him with you?' the officer continued.

'No. She never discussed her personal things with me, though I wish she had. She was an introvert and hence never shared anything with me. And nor did I. But she did treat me like a younger sister.' Aleesha was trying to play safe while simultaneously answering all their questions to the best of her ability. Otherwise she knew she could land herself up in trouble.

'How was her usual behaviour after consuming alcohol? I mean, did she ever get aggressive?'

'Yes. Almost every time. Otherwise she would simply go off to sleep,' Aleesha replied.

The officer told both of them that they were not permitted to move out from the city until the investigation went on and they had to be present whenever he called them. They both got up to leave. As they walked outside the police station separately, the feeling of betrayal overcame them.

Aleesha felt betrayed by Akash while he felt betrayed by his colleagues and Tamanna. He didn't want Aleesha to know about everything like this. He wanted to explain to her that he was not wrong and seriously loved her. He had just told the truth to avoid Aleesha from being apprehensive about him going to office. He never wanted Tamanna to know about his relationship initially since he knew she had a huge crush on him, and he feared losing job. He was sure that if Aleesha came to know that Tamanna and he worked together, she wouldn't be able to hide it from her. He had done everything for Aleesha. He was innocent and was afraid of losing her from the very first day they met. After all, he had loved someone so deeply after a very long time and wanted this relationship to last and culminate into marriage. He wanted it to last forever. But fate had some other plan from him.

Aleesha was hurt, not just because Akash had lied to her, but because she believed that he had shattered her trust by being sexually attracted towards Tammy and forcing her to make out with him. After they had covered a fairly long distance from the police station, Akash turned to her with pleading eyes, only to be told, 'How could you play with me like this? Why would you not tell me the truth? If it was over, you should have set me free. How could you force yourself on Tammy di, play with her feelings, and drag me along when you knew you were completely wrong! I believed you and never thought you would lie or leave me like this but now I know you were playing cheap games with Tammy di as well as me. I thought I could never hate you but I was wrong. You know what I really can't believe—the mere fact that I believed you.'

Akash stood there numbly, with tears rolling down. He just stared at Aleesha who walked away from him, got into a bus, and left. She didn't even wait for a clarification from him.

He felt it was all over. Once the trust has been broken, it's broken. It may grow back a bit, but it'll never be the same as before. This end was not the way he wanted it, but he was helpless.

Everything He Did, He Did It For Her

'Where are you, Aditya?' Akash seemed worried. I guessed something was wrong.

'What happened? You were not in office today. How did Tamanna leave you alone?' I joked.

'Shut up Aditya! I am screwed. Tamanna is no more. She is dead and the police is accusing me of her death. I have called you from a PCO near the police station.'

Oh fuck! I thought he was kidding but he was fucking serious. He told me the entire story, leaving me utterly speechless. I was facing such a situation for the first time in my life where the police had caught hold of one of my best friends. I was completely blank, and didn't know how to react. I acted as a mere spectator and agreed to whatever he said. We decided to meet at DP restaurant in Matunga. He asked me to convince Aleesha to join us. Akash had left for office directly from the police station. He was regretting throwing away his cell the previous night. Had he not reacted in anger, he would have been able to message Aleesha expressing what he felt at that moment. He rushed to the office immediately to get another shock of his life.

'Deep, we are extremely sorry but the authorities have sent us an email regarding your termination,' said Mr Verma handing him a copy of the email and informing him that a soft copy of the mail had been forwarded to him.

'The board members feel that though they are sorry about Tamanna's untimely death, the matter in which she died is still unknown and since your name is being investigated in this case, they can't retain such employees. This is their final decision. I am sorry,' Mr Verma explained.

The world rotates once every 24 hours but for Akash it had rotated more than 24 times in the last 24 hours. His world had turned upside down in a matter of a single day. He had least expected that there was no client meeting the previous evening, that and it was all a planned game by Tamanna. He had run away from that situation to land up in bigger trouble. He wouldn't have imagined that the next day when he would reach office, the police would be waiting for him to investigate Tamanna's death. But the climax was yet to come. The termination letter was handed over to him for the misconduct of policies.

It was all so crazy! Who could have imagined all this to happen within a span of 24 hours? It was like a Snakes and Ladders game in which you are almost at the top when you are suddenly bitten by a snake at the 98th position and come crashing down. All his dreams had been shattered in one go. He cried all the way to Matunga. He reached DP's restaurant and didn't have to wait for long for us to arrive. Aleesha was first reluctant to come inside but I convinced her somehow. Aleesha didn't even look at Akash and I felt like a mediator between them.

'Why have you brought me here? I came for you, not for this big time cheat,' Aleesha screamed on seeing Akash.

'Aleesha, calm down please. I request you not to create scene here,' pleaded Akash.

'Oh, is it? Then I better leave as I am one slut who creates a scene everywhere. However, you are the most decent guy ever who never misbehaves with anyone.'

I calmed her down and told her not to be so hyper about things and asked her to hear Akash out first before making any judgements. I held her hand to make her feel better. She looked extremely pale, like she would faint any moment. I felt pity on her but I also knew that it was not Akash's fault. But as they say, everything that is destined to happen will happen and we can't change it.

'Jaan, my Minnie, how can you even think that I will double date you or play with your feelings? We can't choose our parents or children, we accept them and love them with all our hearts. But my Minnie, I chose you because my heart liked you and I felt that you are what I want, and I want to love you for a lifetime! The day I saw you at Thrive Club, I felt some strange connection with you. I had a bet with Aditya that I would talk to you for at least a few minutes. In those few minutes, you stole my heart. We had just started conversing when you disclosed that you lived here with your family friend 'Tamanna Kapoor' who worked as a manager at Galaxy House. Before I could speak, I saw Tamanna walking towards us from afar. I hurriedly left before she could see me with you. Not because I wanted to hide my identity from you or her, but because I knew she had a secret crush on me. I thought being with you at that moment could not only screw my professional life but also my personal life. Thus, I decided not to tell you my middle name. I mean no one calls me Deep except for some of my colleagues in office. Some even called me Akashdeep during my college days and I hated it. But everyone including my family members and closed ones call me Akash as that was the name my dad had kept and everyone knows that I was my dad's favourite. I don't use two names to fool people. I wanted to be your friend or maybe more than a friend. When you didn't come to meet me the next day, I thought it was because Tammy had seen us and told you not to get involved with me. But I soon realized that it was nothing like that. I was in love. I thought of telling Tamanna about us so that I could visit your house regularly. My fortune favoured me and I got a chance to be with Tamanna alone in the office one day when the system failed. It was going to take time to reinstall, and we had to stay in office till late at night. I thought that was the perfect moment to tell her but what I saw that night left me stunned. She had gone to bring coffee for us from the vending machine. I thought of having a smoke and went outside. When I went near the vending machine, I heard some noises and I peeped from the passage. Tamanna was fantasizing in front of coffee vending machine and I could clearly hear her moaning my name. I was shocked and soon realized that it was not just a simple crush. I dropped my plan to tell Tamanna about us, ran back to the work floor, and sat in my chair, pretending nothing had happened,' Akash explained.

'I also want to tell you that I never lied about my company to you. Though I work for Galaxy House, I I get my basic salary from RS Group as I am on their payroll which is called third party payroll. I will be shifted to another site once the project is over. My offer letter, my email id, my I-card, and all other official documents are in the name of RS Group. However, my HRA, bonus, PF, and all other benefits come from Galaxy House, which were all in Tamanna's hands. That was the only reason why I had to be nice with her. Otherwise I had no interest in even looking at her. Thus, I didn't tell her anything that night. I am the only earning member of my family and I can't be aggressive without thinking of the consequences. I couldn't afford to lose this reputed job due to recession and because there were no new openings in the market. Yes, I purposely never told you about my current office after that incident because I feared losing you. I had not only thought of telling you about my company but also wanted to introduce you to my family. I also wanted to tell you my middle name in spite of knowing that you stay with my manager, Tamanna. But the coffee incident made me think otherwise. I had no choice else she would have continued playing her dirty games on me. Trust me on this. It was always her staring at me when I went near her desk or when she tried to come close to me during parties and office conferences, I would call Aditya from the office and tell him about it immediately.. The only thing I regret is not telling Aditya about the last client meeting. I have really pictured you as my wife and can't imagine you going away from my life because of some third person who was obsessed about me,' he continued.

Akash even narrated the entire Panvel incident once again to let Aleesha know that he never fooled her and was loyal even when he could have used Tamanna to climb the ladder of success. Nevertheless, Aleesha had a different opinion on it and was not in a frame of mind where she could easily forgive Akash.

'Aditya, should I leave? I am not interested in listening to his clarifications. I need a break. I can't take it anymore. Not after knowing the truth behind Tamanna di's death,' she said looking at me.

'If I didn't love you, I could have screwed you by informing the police officers about Tamanna's call last night. She told me everything and I trust her. She would never lie to me as she treated me like her sister. You killed her. You are responsible for the whole mess. You deserve nothing better. At least try to be honest to yourself. And if you can't then go away! Get lost. I am breaking all the promises and this relationship, which you never respected but just pretended to be in. You are such a b******. Fuck off. You'll pay for your deeds one day,' she screamed at Akash.

It's not the goodbye that hurts; it's the flashback that follows. It hurts the most when the person who made you feel so special till yesterday, suddenly makes you feel so unwanted today. Aleesha still loved Akash, but she just didn't believe in him anymore. She left. Maybe, forever. Akash had lost everything in last 24 hours.

I Love You So Much, It Hurts

Why is that we recognize love only when it ends? Love never dies a natural death; it dies because of betrayals. Doctors don't operate on these wounds and once it starts bleeding, it causes instant death. The death of love!

'I just wanted her to smile and not doubt me because of what Tamanna had told her. If she had known earlier, it would have ended long back. I wish I could have told Tamanna earlier but I didn't want her to hurt Aleesha in the process. It's my bad luck that not only have I hurt Tamanna and been the cause of her death, but I will probably have to also end my relationship with Aleesha,' Akash muttered to himself.

Akash was walking through the Cyprus area of Mulund when he saw a couple sitting on the same bench where he had spent an evening with Aleesha. All of a sudden, those memories flashed before his eyes—the day when Aleesha had worn a Kashmiri suit that that he had gifted her.

He recollected what Aleesha had told him—'You are the reason for this smile and the glow on my face. I don't need any beauty parlours for this glow. Your kisses make my face glow even in the saddest of moments. Never break my trust, Akash. Just be the same always.'

Walking back home alone , depressed, and frustrated, he cursed God for everything as he had not got what he wanted from life.

'That's not fair. How could you do this to me? Aren't you satisfied with my pain? When I wanted my father around during my growing up years, you took him away from me. I had to convince myself saying, "Akash, you can't be like others. You don't have a dad who can sit beside you when you fail in an exam or who will shout at you when you smoke. You are all alone." Then you brought Aleesha into my life and allowed me to share all my feelings with her. It felt like magic. But suddenly you caught hold of me and kicked me again by making me realize that I am not meant to love anyone. I was alone and will always live like that. If my friend had done all this, I would have asked him why was he doing this to me? But, how should I ask you? You are the Almighty. It's okay. You carry on.'

He had called her more than a hundred times from his alternate mobile number but did not get a response. She kept ignoring all his calls. Finally he sent her a message:

You really feel I am a liar? Even when I lied to you that I was not drinking with my friends, you caught me. Was I ever successful in lying to you? Then how can you just walk away like this without giving me a second chance? I don't know how to put this across to you, but I would like you to know that you were, you are, and you will always remain my princess. I know I didn't tell you things which I should have told `you a long time ago, but... How could you even think like that? It was just you with whom I shared my little secrets. Even when I cut my nails, I told you. So at least you should have given me a second chance. But, I know these words mean nothing to you as you have lost your trust in me and don't want to hear any more clarifications. Maybe, I shouldn't have come into your life and raised your hopes, only to shatter them. But falling in love with you was not in my hands. How many times have I told you not to make decisions in haste? But...`

He waited for a reply but knew that she wouldn't. She had already assumed that he was the villain of the story. Akash was devastated and couldn't believe that he had lost his job, his respect, his self-confidence, and his love—all in one go. Akash felt as helpless as a puppet in destiny's hand and however hard he tried to break from its clutches, he was unable to do it. The only good thing was that Kritika firmly stood by him in this time of crisis like a good friend. She believed in him and wanted Aleesha and Akash to be together once again.

The next morning, Akash went to her hostel and waited under the same tree where he had once waited for her before going on a date. This time he waited there to make Aleesha realize what reality was. Kritika messaged him that Aleesha had left the room, so he went closer to the main gate. He turned nervous when he saw Aleesha coming towards him. She seemed to have cried a lot and she had even forgotten to put her eyeliner, and there were bags under her eyes. Aleesha saw Akash, but she completely ignored him and walked ahead. Akash had made up his mind that he would talk with her anyhow. He ran behind her and stopped her midway.

'What's this? You could at least hear what I have to say. You are not even taking my calls or replying to my messages.'

'Look Akash, please don't irritate me like this, or I will scream. Go away. I don't want to hear anything. I trusted you and felt you were different from other guys who just plays with the emotions of girls. But I was wrong. All guys are the same. Tamanna was right. I wish she had warned me before. At least her parents wouldn't have suffered. You killed her parents too. They have lost their sole reason to live. Even my parents are... Forget it, why am I telling you all this? You are a loser. Go away.'

'Do you even know why I did that? I lost my job. I knew something of this sort would happen once Tammy came to know about us. She was one obsessed girl. She behaved like a...'

'Oh please! Don't use such words for her. You think I'll listen to your lies again? Buzz off. Yes, you said it right. I shouldn't have assumed you were different from others, Mr Akash, or should I call you Mr Deep? You are... you knew that we are family friends and still you forced her... Go away Akash. Don't force me to shout and create a scene here.'

That was it! Akash had lost his one final chance too. Aleesha was in no mood to hear him out. She had never witnessed the death of a closed one before. It was the biggest shock of her life and the parental pressure to come back to Kolkata was making her head spin. But she had to wait until the cops allowed her to leave the city. The medical reports were yet to come and she had to wait. Akash wondered how Aleesha could get over their relationship so easily. He checked his recent updates on BBM and saw Aleesha's status update.

I am not ignoring you but just trying to lessen my expectations from you and preventing myself from being hurt again.

Akash messaged her immediately…

Not even for one night can I sleep without thinking about you. And you have no idea how loudly my heart beats for you. Don't crush it so harshly. We may have to part ways for now, but you will always be the one for me.

'She doesn't even talk about me once?' Akash asked Kritika. We were all at Shivaji Park, Dadar.

'She does. But she is too disturbed and… How should I tell you? She has lost trust in you completely,' Kritika answered.

'Aditya, am I that bad? You think I can really play with her feelings? Tamanna has screwed it all. She is not even in this world anymore to clear the mess. How can I prove to Aleesha that I am innocent? I don't care about the cops but…this is the same place where she had consulted me about shifting to a hostel and today she kicked me out of her life without even consulting me, ' Akash said with watery eyes.

Almost a week had passed and the situation had only worsened. Kritika and I were consoling him and trying to bring him out of depression. Kritika even tried to convince Aleesha but it was of no use. After I tricked her into meeting Akash, she ignored me as well. All we could do was to be with Akash and make him feel better. Kritika even missed her lectures and supported Akash. This gesture made him feel better since Kritika was Aleesha's friend. She knew misunderstandings do happen and was positive about their patch up. Her amethyst crystal made her feel so. But nowhere could we see any light of hope.

'Akash, I would suggest you wait for the medical reports. Tomorrow, the medical reports will be with the police and then the picture will be clear to us. Aleesha will be convinced after that but till then don't be sad. I know how it feels. You know what I went through. Even this phase will pass. Trust me,' I tried to motivate him.

Akash felt like his body was being ripped apart into half. The medical reports were yet to come. They were his only hope to prove himself innocent. He couldn't sleep the entire night, the same way a student can't sleep the night before his Viva especially when he is the target of all the professors who are waiting to pounce upon him. The mere thought of the police station made him nervous.

The next morning when he reached the police station, Aleesha was already there, sitting in front of the officer. Her eyes were wet but her mind was firm. The officer glanced through the reports.

'This is the medical report which we were waiting for. And as expected, it makes everything clear,' the officer said.

Akash crossed his fingers and bit his teeth in nervousness. Nothing had gone right in the last few days and the blame game by colleagues had left a deep impact on him. Inspite of being loyal to Aleesha, he was sitting beside her in the police station like a stranger.

'We are closing the case. The medical reports say that percentage of alcoholic content was way above the permitted limit in her body. She was not in a state to drive. There were no marks found on her body. This clears the doubt of rape and sexual harassment. It was just an accident. I am sorry for all the trouble you had to go through but that's our duty. You can leave, you are free now,' the officer announced.

Akash's happiness knew no bounds. As they walked farther away from the police station, Akash stopped Aleesha midway and gave her big smile.

'Stop it Akash. You are...' Aleesha screamed which turned many heads in their direction.

'Now what? Didn't you hear what the officer said? It was an accident. The intake of alchohol killed her, not me. I didn't force myself upon her. There are no marks on her body. He said this very clearly. Now trust me jaan,' Akash pleaded.

'You think I was waiting for the reports to come? You are wrong, Mr Akash. There are so many cases that get shut due to lack of evidence, but the real truth is known only to the family members. So what if there are no marks on her body? You must have done it with her on a previous occasion. Otherwise why would Tammy di lie to me? She said it very clearly that you lusted for her and had always wanted to take her to bed with you. Why would she try to spoil our relationship? If she would have known that we loved each other, she would have been happy for us. Anyway, let's not discuss this any further. It's over between us.'

'Aleesha please don't do this to me. I agree that I should have told you, but I did all that for you. I never...'

Everytime he tried to speak, Aleesha stopped him short. She kept walking away from him as if he was a stranger. When Akash stopped following her, she turned back and said:

'Akash, I will never say I regret being with you. Because at one point of time, you were exactly the person I wanted to be with. The past is never a mistake if you have learnt from it. I have learnt never to trust someone so much that it hurts your expectations. Even I never wanted it to end this way. It's all your fault. I don't want to take revenge or teach you a lesson, but you will bear the consequences of your actions by losing me. Bye Akash. I am changing my number.'

'You are again assuming things and not looking at the other side of the coin, Aleesha...' Akash screamed after her. But this time she didn't turn back.

'Aleesha, where are you going? What have I done to you that you have stopped discussing things with me?' Kritika enquired when she saw Aleesha packing her bags.

'You think I am a fool? As if I don't know that you are busy running after Akash. I'm not blind. It's better to be calculative rather than regret later,' Aleesha exclaimed.

'Oh please! You all are just my friends and it's my responsibility to be with my friends when they need me. I am tired of making you understand. Can't you give him one chance?' Kritika added.

'Why should I? So that he breaks my heart and insults my love again? And you don't need to tell me what responsibility is. I won't be surprised to see you both on this very bed when I return from Kolkata. Tamanna failed to warn me earlier, but I am warning you in advance,' Aleesha screamed, making Kritika lose her temper.

Aleesha's parents too were upset and wanted her to come back to Kolkata for a week or two as there were no lectures due to college functions. Aleesha also needed a change. Though she still loved Akash more than anything in the world, she was afraid to start everything all over again since it was difficult for her to live with the fact that Tammy had died because of Akash's harassment. Her subconscious mind never believed that Akash could have harassed Tammy but she couldn't ignore Tamanna's last phone call either.

As soon as Kritika told Akash that Aleesha was leaving for Kolkata, he couldn't stop himself from going to the airport to convince her for the last time. But she had already checked-in and Akash didn't find her anywhere near the departure gates. He couldn't deal with all the pain and wanted to end it but had no clue whatsoever. Sometimes he wondered if anybody would miss him even if he put a bullet through his head, sometimes he wondered why it started when it had to end this way. The world kept crumbling around him. All his hopes had vanished. He had to convince his heart that it had ended for good. But whenever he stood in front of the mirror, he saw this person getting tortured. He watched this other Akash suffer all the pain and crying to sleep every night with a wish that this suffering would end. But it kept growing inside him, killing him bit by bit every day. So what was his destiny?

To walk on the path of sorrow and pain?

What an Idea, Sirji!

February 13

A month had passed since Tamanna's death but the wounds were still fresh. There are times when you feel nothing could possibly favour you. Akash was sitting alone, trying hard to get past the emptiness he felt within his soul, but was lost, scared, and couldn't feel pleasant about anything around him.

One death had scattered many lives. Her parents, Aleesha, Akash, Kritika, and me—all had suffered the pain of loss. Aleesha had lost trust in Akash and Kritika had lost a friend in Aleesha, while Akash had lost everything.

Still time doesn't stop for anyone and life moves on.

It was February 13, Kritika's birthday!

She had forced Akash and me to join the party organized by her friends in Lavasa. Despite our constant pleading, Kritika had managed to convince us both to come. We were staying at Ekaant Hotel which had an amazing view of the valley. We were sad but tried our best to hide our sadness from others at the venue. Kritika's college friends were also present at that time. Akash tried to hide his feelings as he didn't want to spoil

Kritika's party. She had supported him selflessly during the bad times. However, it was difficult for him to attended the party and pretend like nothing had happened.

I brought him a plate of biryani but he refused to eat.

I knew how it felt to go through such a difficult phase. Though your face shows no expressions, your soul is deeply tormented.

'Kritika, did Aleesha call you?' Akash enquired.

'Yes. We even chatted for some time. She is returning back from Kolkata tomorrow,' Kritika answered.

'Did she talk about me even once? Please tell me…'

Akash was getting on my nerves by continuously talking about Aleesha.

'We chatted on WhatsApp yesterday so I can mail that to you. Give me your mail id,' Kritika replied.

I was drunk and losing my patience.

'Haaa, the same way you would mail me all of that bitch Tamanna's chats. Tamanna did this, Tamanna did that, Tammy looked at me, Tammy tried to fuck me, blah blah blah… All your WhatsApp conversations are still fucking lying in my Gmail account which I hardly check. Get over it, Akash. Don't be a coward. What did I ever do with the chats you sent? Nothing. So what are you going to do with Kritika and Aleesha's chat? Kritika at least you should know better…' I screamed.

Suddenly, I stopped dead in my tracks. I still had Tamanna and Akash's WhatsApp chats saved on my Gmail account!

'Akash, my mailbox! You have mailed me all the WhatsApp chats you had with Tamanna. Do you remember even one which one can help prove to Aleesha that you are innocent.' I screamed aloud in excitement.

'Oh my God, that's amazing! And if you don't find anything relevant, then you can put up a request to the service provider to retrieve your messages. We have finally found a way out of this mess,' Kritika shrieked and jumped in excitement.

'I don't remember my password now but it's saved on my system. So let's check it once we reach Mumbai tomorrow morning. What say guys?' I added.

All three of us jumped in joy and high-fived each other. Akash hugged me with tears in his eyes. We had found a ray of hope that could bring new sunshine into Akash's life. The charm on his face was back. We all wished that we could find the relevant chats which could convince Aleesha that Tamanna was a liar and wanted to destroy her relationship with Akash.

'You both have given me hope for a better tomorrow,' Akash exclaimed in happiness and continued, 'I never meant to cause her trouble. I owe so much to her. Now that I have a way, I know we will be together again and live for each other until life closes its last curtain.'

He hoped that they will unite again on the day of love—February 14.

Never Knew Love Like This

February 14

The new dawn had brought with it new rays of hope in Akash's life. He was so excited to see Aleesha after such a long period of time that he didn't even bother changing his clothes in the morning. He was nervous and excited at the same time. Just thinking about Aleesha's touch brought the dimples back on his face. As soon as we reached Mumbai, Akash, without even caring to return back home, directly came to my house to check my mails.

'Aadi, log in fast. Please.' He sounded excited.

'What do you think I am I doing? Watching porn? At least give me a minute to check,' I told him.

As we waited for my Gmail account to open, I went to quickly freshen up otherwise my mom would have logged me out of the house. Once open, Akash carefully searched all the mails in my inbox. He opened every mail with the subject: WhatsApp Chat with Tamanna, and transferred them to his cell phone. He scanned my entire Inbox and even opened the trash and spam folders to make sure that he had not missed out on any mail.

'Aadiiiiii...Aadiiii, come here quickly.' he screamed as if the house had been set on fire.'

I was in the middle of a shower when he yelled and I had to come out running half naked with a towel wrapped around me and shampoo still in my hair. 'Look at this mail,' Akash pointed to the computer screen.

'Chat history is attached as "WhatsApp Chat with Tammy.txt" to this email.'

I checked the time and date again. January 13, 11.30 pm.

Holy shit! It was sent on the same day Tamanna's accident! It means Akash had mailed me their last WhatsApp conversation. Now who the hell checks the spam folders!

'How did this mail go into spam?' I asked.

'I had sent it from my new id. Fuck, I wish we could have seen this earlier!' said Akash scratching his head.

I was dumbstruck after reading the message and cursed myself. If he had mailed me from his frequently used id, it wouldn't have gone in spam. We stared at each other after reading the entire chat. This time we both screamed in pleasure and hugged each other. Akash wanted to go over to Aleesha's place that very instant and show her all the chats between Tamanna and himself which would prove not only his innocence but also prove how much he loved Aleesha. He couldn't hold it any longer and ran to Aleesha to make her fall in love with him all over again.

Suddenly love was back in his life. He wasn't perfect and neither was Aleesha. Perfect couples don't exist, but there is always someone who is perfect for you. Akash ran to meet his imperfectly perfect love Aleesha!

He boarded the local train to CST, remembering how he had boarded the ladies compartment when they had fought for the first time after she caught him staring at the girl's poster. In the entire one-hour journey to her house, Aleesha's thoughts kept lingering in his mind. Distance really makes the heart grow fonder. All the incidents that had seemed irritating at that time, now seemed cute to him when he thought of them. Separation from a loved one makes you realize their worth. Akash wanted to surf on the ocean of love. When he got down at CST, he called Kritika to enquire about Aleesha. Kritika told him that she had gone to Tamanna's apartment to collect something. He immediately took a taxi to Tamanna's apartment. Once he reached there, his mind went back to the time he had dropped Tamanna home after the party. Back then, he had never thought his life would take such a U-turn that he would lose everything. He wiped tears from his cheeks to make way for happiness.

When a girl cries over a guy, it means that she misses him. But when a guy cries over a girl, it means that no one else can love that girl more than he does. Akash not only shed tears but he also did everything possible to bring her back into his life. Now standing at the entrance of her apartment, he had goosebumps all over. He took a deep breath and pressed the bell.

He closed his eyes for a few seconds and thought of what lay ahead. He had waited for this moment. His days were clouded with her thoughts and nights rained with her dreams. He prayed hard to bring her back. When he opened his eyes, Aleesha was standing in front of him, staring.

He was speechless. It doesn't matter if the person you love the most has broken your heart or been the cause of your sleeplessness, but when you see that person after so many days, your heart still misses a beat. Akash was numb seeing Aleesha after so many days. He smiled at her warmly.

'Why don't you leave me alone?' Aleesha screamed and pleaded him to go away even though in her heart, she wanted him to stay. It made her feel better after seeing him, but she couldn't forget the sadness she saw in Tamanna's dad's eyes when she visited her folks in Kolkata.

She was just about to shut the door when Akash forcefully stepped in. Without wasting a minute, he sat on the sofa and started speaking,

'Aleesha, I love you. Today, seeing you after so many days...' 'Akash why are you here?' Aleesha interrupted him.

'I want to show you something which will make you believe that I'm innocent and had nothing to do with Tamanna's death. Not only that, I will also prove to you that I never encouraged Tamanna to come near me and always stayed away from her…'

'Akash, please, don't start this all over again. I don't want to listen to any of your stories. If you want to convince me that what you're saying is true, then the only way to prove it is by bringing Tamanna in front of me and that's impossible. So chuck it. You better…'

'That's what I am going to do. I mean, I can't bring her in front of you, but I can show you her chats. Yes, I used to mail all the chats she had with me on WhatsApp to Aditya. If I would have remembered this earlier, I would have proven myself innocent long ago. Even when I left the farmhouse that night, I had messaged her. So that should clear all your doubts. Read this and you will believe that Tammy wanted us to part ways and break our relationship,' said Akash handing her his mobile phone.

He urged her to read that night's conversation first and then the others. Aleesha looked at Akash. She was confused, for she didn't know whether to believe Tammy di or Akash. The innocence in his eyes told her that he had nothing to do with Tamanna's death and that he still loved her. Even Aleesha hoped Akash was innocent. She was equally nervous when Akash urged her to read the messages.

10.15 pm, 13 Jan, Tammy: Akash, please come back. I need you, not beside me but above me. Please don't leave me alone. You never looked at me but I always felt some connection with you and now you are leaving me here unsatisfied—what for? For that bitch Aleesha? That bloody slut can't take you away from me.

10.18 pm, 13 Jan, Akash: I told you everything. I am sorry but I love Aleesha a lot. So stop trying your luck with me. I am not your puppet, Ms Tamanna Kapoor. Try respecting at least the girl who treats you like an elder sister.

10.20 pm, 13 Jan, Tammy: You are ignoring my requests? How can you? Come back right now or you will have to face the consequences. I will make sure you are mine. If you can't be mine, then I'll make sure you can't be with anyone else too. I'll make you beg for my love. I'll make sure you lose everything you have and come back to me so that I can give you everything you want... Till then, fuck that bitch.

10.25 pm, 29 Mar, Tammy: <Media omitted>

10.26 pm, 29 Mar, Tammy: <Media omitted>

10.27 pm, 29 Mar, Tammy: <Media omitted>

10.28 pm, 29 Mar - Tammy: Keep ignoring me and I will send you more such photos. You have to come back to me. You can't go away like this. I will prove to you that I am better than her.

She looked at Akash with teary eyes and asked:

'What's this "Media omitted"?'

'Her photographs. Not exactly naked ones, but ones in which she is skimpily dressed. She tried her best to make me go back to the farmhouse. She tried forcing herself on me, pressurizing me, and seducing me. But everything failed. I ignored her messages after trying to convince her that I love you a lot. But when she started sending me photographs, I decided to send her one last and final message. After that, she started to call me continuously and I threw away my phone in frustration.'

Aleesha continued reading:

11.50 pm, 13 Jan, Akash: You do whatever you feel like and I'll do what I feel is right. These photographs won't affect me. My soul, my heart belongs only to Aleesha and I can't hurt her. I know such behaviour can devastate you and maybe you'll start hating me, but I can't help it. We can't keep everyone around us happy. My only aim in life is to keep Aleesha happy and make my family proud of me by achieving `success without taking the shortcut. I can never be yours and you can never make me yours. It will be better if you get over me ASAP. Bye.`

After reading the entire conversation, Aleesha started sobbing. She continued reading other chats that had occured between them before that night and realized that Akash was actually telling the truth. She couldn't believe Tammy had played such a dirty game on her. She hated herself for not trusting Akash, for taking decisions in haste, and for assuming things without even thinking twice. She felt guilty for having treated Akash so badly in the last few days, yet he was sitting in front of her with the same love in his eyes as before. Akash went closer to her, took her hands in his, and hugged her, as he understood the pain that Aleesha felt somewhere deep inside her after reading everything. After some time, she freed herself from his arms abruptly.

'But…how could she speak such crap… I still don't believe that she could have…is it some trick…?' she tried to speak but every touch of Akash made her weak. Akash had held her tightly by her waist and was circling his fingers on her lower back, slowly working his way up, and Aleesha was finding it hard to resist.

'Akash, I am still confused…don't do this to me. You are making me…aahhh!' she moaned as he rubbed her back and tried to pull down her shorts.

'Aleesha…don't stop me. It's been so long and I have missed you so much. Now at least believe me that I was not wrong. Let's forget everything! Come close to me, jaan. Come very close,' he muttered kissing her ears and biting them tenderly.

She kept moaning in pleasure and her resistance decreased with every kiss. He was about to kiss her on the lips when she said, 'Not here. This room doesn't have curtains. Let's go inside in bedroom.'

She stopped all the accusations and simply accepted that Akash could turn her on with ease. Her body throbbed for his touch once again.

Akash lifted her and she closed her eyes and held on to him tightly. He took her inside one of the bedrooms and put her on the bed. He pounced on her, kissing her all over her body.

'This is Tammy's room,' Aleesha said in response to Akash's passionate smooch.

'So what? It has a bed and here you are in front of my eyes longing for love,' Akash responded. The next moment, they had ripped each other's clothes apart.

Her face looked radiant while her body swirled in passion as Akash kissed every inch of her. Akash talked dirty as he gazed at her as if he was seeing her for the first time.

Aleesha was spread out on the bed sheet with Akash on top of her, making sweet love to her. But something under the bed sheet kept irking her.

'Akash I can feel something under me,' she said trying to reach out for it.

He removed the bed sheet and found a pen drive. Aleesha recognized it as being Tamanna's. Akash was fortunately carrying his laptop with him so Aleesha plugged the pen drive in the USB port.

'How disgusting is this. Don't kill the mood,' Akash teased her but she ignored him. The pen drive contained only one folder named 'Akash'. The folder contained a number of documents.

'Oh fuck! I remember she used to always note down something on her Galaxy Tab,' Akash remembered the incident in the taxi when Tamanna had read a few lines for him.

More shocking were the contents of the documents—it was like Tamanna's personal diary of sorts. Each word in the document left them stunned, not because of the contents alone, but because they had trusted a completely wrong person, and the extent of her obsession not only astounded them but also left them thinking how a girl could be so infatuated with someone. Her fantasies knew no bounds. One of the lines read:

Agar tujhko naa paa saki, toh zindagi na rahegi baaki,

Agar tu mera na ho paaya, toh mujhse peecha kahan jaayega chudaake!

Aana toh tujhe phir yahin hai, kyunki mere bina teri zindagi kahan poori hai!

Aa choo le mere jawaani ko, varna kya naam doongi apni kahaani ko!

Akash kept thinking whether it was corporate boredom that led her to behave like this or was it just pure lust? Before Aleesha's mood could change form happy to glum, Akash told her to ignore the contents of the pen drive since the truth was out in the open and they had finally been united. They continued with their love making session. This time it was more intense than before since Aleesha was now completely convinced that Akash was right and could never betray her for someone else.

'You bring out the best in me. I feel as if I could grow wings and kiss the clouds. You're my wickedly wonderful baby. I love you. You are mine! Just mine! And am all yours... I missed this so much. Now I feel complete,' said Aleesha and hugged him.

She wanted to give him everything that she could not give in last few days...Love...romance...kisses...hugs... everything! They kissed each other all over. They truly believed they were meant to be together.

As a couple, you will have to go through life's various struggles. But in the end, everything will pass. And if it doesn't, it's not the end.

It started with a friend request...and life was never the same again.

Epilogue

Almost a year has passed since Tamanna's death and Akash is now working as a Team leader in a renowned company in South Mumbai. He has even set up a small online business from which he generates a healthy income. There's no lack of money for him now. Along with financial success, he has also been able to build long-term relationships with people through his charming personality and professional conduct.

Aleesha and Kritika patched up after their big fight and are now BFFs again. They share almost everything with each other, except boyfriends. Kritika now concentrates more on BMS books, but she is still fond of *Cosmopolitan* magazine and reads it every night. She has still not found a guy who can cook for her but her Amethyst crystal helps spread positivity in her life and she is sure she will strike it lucky with love one day.

Mr Verma still works at Galaxy house and he still loves to be surrounded with girls half his age, but Kajal has resigned from her job and is searching for a better one. She finally understood that even Mr Verma could screw her the same way Tammy screwed Akash's life. She realized that taking shortcuts can make you achieve your short-term goals but can't make you win life's marathon.

Aleesha's family is now chilled about their daughter as she scored good grades in her examination. They are also quite cool about her relationship with Akash. However, the Kapoor family is heartbroken after Tamanna's death. They are still not over it and cannot digest that their daughter is no more in this world to support them in their old age. Only if Tamanna had controlled her aggression that day, she would still be alive. She was not killed in an accident. The feelings of jealousy, revenge, and obsession had killed her slowly each day until she was finally declared dead by the world. When Akash and Aleesha found her pen drive, they realized that her obsession was beyond anyone's imagination. Respecting her feelings, Akash has told me not to write about the notes from the pen drive.

What about Aditya?

Well, what can happen to me? In my life, I've lived. I've loved, I've lost, I've missed, I've hurt. I've trusted, I've made mistakes, but most of all, I've learned. I still crave for my true love. But now we are like two parallel lines which can never meet, but at least will be together after death. However, I found true best friends in Kritika and Aleesha—friends who are hard to find, difficult to leave, and impossible to forget! We still hang out together and look out for each other in bad times. Life would never have been the same without them. When I look back and review the Tamanna and Akash episode, it teaches me to be careful about the people I deal with on an everyday basis and also about the importance of honesty in relationships.

Akash and Aleesha love each other more than before. Sometimes you have to be away from people you love, but that doesn't make you love them less instead it makes you love them more. They even visited Haji Ali after their patch up as they believed that the supreme power had showered blessings on them. After all, life won't give you a second chance like Akash. Don't love the person who is there to have a good time with you! Love the person who really suffers for you because that is true love.

'Akash, when will you stop with your cheap acts? We are already late for the movie and here you are watching porn videos on your mobile. Get over it. You always make me lose my temper and then say that I start fighting,' Aleesha screamed.

'Oh come on. What can I do? I was looking for show timings. The site itself has this advertisement,' Akash defended himself.

'Shut up. Don't act innocent with me and try to fool me.'

'What? Do I shout at you when you read those dirty magazines?' Akash replied.

'Stop it now…'

'Why? Why now when it comes to you?'

And the fight continued…until they sealed it with a kiss.

This is not a story of miracle, this is not a story of revenge, and this is not a story of perfect romance…it's a simple story of love. Love that lasts forever... If you truly love someone and are destined to meet, then you just need to hang in there and wait for the right moment. Their wait was over and they loved each other forever and ever.

Acknowledgements

Amazing things have happened since the release of *Few Things Left Unsaid* (2011) and *That's the Way We Met* (2012). I would like to thank my millions of readers all over the world for their unflinching love and support. You all mean a lot to me!

All the people that I thank below have been my pillars of strength while I finished writing the manuscript—guiding me, criticizing me, and improving me along the way. I hope their efforts pay off.

I thank Akash, Aleesha, and Kritika, and that moment in Goa when Aleesha convinced me to write about her love story with all its imperfections. The idea struck us when we were lazying on the beach and Kritika suddenly exclaimed, 'Somebody should seriously think about scripting our lives. It's so filmy!' Thank you for convincing me to give it a shot. I hope I have done justice to your story.

I thank Saurabh More for convincing Akash to reveal the truth, even though he feared his mom would be against it. Eventually, we convinced his mom too! Love you Kaki.

This book wouldn't have been possible without the support of Aisha Shah who stood by me even when her son Mohsin was writing his exams.

To Mrunmayee, for handling my mood swings. You are a sweetheart! To Dipika Tanna and Reeda Dalwai for reviewing the script at Rajnikanth's pace as many times as I requested them. To Swati Chaure for boosting my morale throughout the journey. To Hetal Bhanushali for helping me finalize the title and Priyanka Dhasade for being her sophisticated self, always.

Thank you to my grandparents—Sulbha and Divakar Palimkar—for your constant support and blessings.

Thanks to Shalini Katyal and Diksha Babbar for being the sweetest friends and motivating me during my rough phase.

Thanks to Zankrut Oza, Narendra Singh, Manik Jaiswal, and RJ Jeeturaaj for their selfless promotions.

To the people who really matter—mom, dad, and my sister Shweta for their humble support. Love you all!

To God, for being kind to me when it comes to my writing.

My extended family on Twitter and Facebook.

Thanks to Milee Ashwarya, Gurveen Chadha, and the entire team at Random house India for always answering my crazy questions.

I am extremely sorry if I have missed out a few names, but each one who is reading this holds a special place in my heart. Love you forever and hamesha!

A Note on the Author

Sudeep Nagarkar is the author of two bestselling novels—*Few Things Left Unsaid* (2011) and *That's the Way We Met* (2012).

Sudeep's books are inspired from real life incidents. They have been translated into regional languages and continue to top the bestseller charts.

He has a degree in Electronics Engineering from Mumbai University and is currently pursuing management studies from Welingkar Institute of Management. He is also a motivational speaker and has given guest lectures in various institutes and organizations. He resides in Mumbai.

You can get in touch with Sudeep via:

Facebook: www.facebook.com/sudeep.nagarkar

Twitter: www.twitter.com/sudeep_nagarkar

Facebook fan page: www.facebook.com/sudeep-nagarkarfanpage

Email: sudeepnagarkar@gmail.com